I0452621

SCREETY

Secret Club Rescuing Every Emotionally Torn Yoni

By Dakota Jack

www.screety.com

Dedication

I dedicate this book to all the women who get up and

fight every day; for happiness, for health, for love,

and simply, for peace. In the words of Tupac Shukar,

"But please don't cry, dry your eyes, never let up.

Forgive, but don't forget, girl, keep your head up."

-Dakota Jack

1

I can't tell you what exactly attracted Greyson to me in the first place. I'm really the furthest thing from his "type." He seems to prefer *amazonish* women; you know, the really tall, really thick and curvy type. Your waist must be cinched, and your hips must be round. And if I had to guess, I'd say you need to be at least five-feet-eight-inches tall or taller. Oh, and if you wear trendy, overly revealing clothes, long glittery nails, a fully made-up face in the daytime, and do your grocery shopping in six-inch heels, even better. You're totally my husband's type.

On the other hand, I'm just an ol' "plain Jane." I'm short, five-feet-one-inch tall, and neither my butt nor boobs protrude with any real significance in either direction. I'm somewhat petite, so no big round hips over here, but I guess my 34-24-34-inch frame gives me a few curves. Since I'm an elementary school teacher, I dress conservatively for the most part. However, on the weekends, a t-shirt and a nice pair of jeans work perfectly fine for me. If asked what I thought was my best physical feature, I'd probably say my hair. It's really long. I haven't cut it in over ten years, just light trims when I go to the salon. Greyson loves my hair; maybe that's what attracted him to me, but he hates that I always keep it pulled up in a bun.

The way I wear my hair isn't the only thing that Greyson seems to hate. Some days, it looks as though he just hates me altogether. I can't even begin to understand why. He's done some things, mean things, which have hurt me to my core. Still, I couldn't pull the plug on my love for him, even if I wanted to. We have been together for eight years and married for two. I've loved Greyson from the very first day we met. I know that sounds ridiculous, but it's true. Maybe I was a little vulnerable or just plain ol' tired of being single, but when he walked over to me at a friend's wedding reception and asked me to dance, I was immediately smitten and have been ever since.

Greyson is a music producer. He's worked with some of everybody. He knows some of everybody; including a shit-load of beautiful, flirty, and amazonish women. He's always in the studio late at night, until crazy hours in the morning, and often in the presence of a woman or women who fit that bill. I hate it. I absolutely hate it. However, I knew his profession from the beginning, and I understand what it entails. I've seen him work to get to where he is today, and I'm so proud of him. And although he's still climbing the industry ranks, he's come a long way, and he takes good care of me, financially at least. He takes good care of us. Lord knows my teacher's salary couldn't come close to securing a lavish condo in Buckhead, but here we are.

Of course, in life, we must be willing to take the good with the bad, and the happy with the sad. But I feel like I've taken more than my share of them both; the bad and sad, that is, particularly as it pertains to my husband.

These emotional roller coaster rides with Greyson took off from the very beginning when he stood me up one week after we met. Greyson and I were supposed to meet downtown at the Westin for dinner and drinks. We had been texting and talking to each other all day, all week long really. I was beyond excited. I got my hair and make-up done and bought a sexy, off-the-shoulder red dress to wear. I was running just a few minutes late, so I text Greyson to let him know. However, by the time I arrived at the restaurant, I realized he never responded, so I gave him a call; no answer.

After sitting at the bar for more than two hours, and blowing up Greyson's phone to no avail, I accepted the fact that he wasn't coming. Humiliated, I paid for my tab, tipped the bartender, and went home. I cried the whole way. Part of me wondered if something bad had happened to him, but my gut was telling me that wasn't the case.

Sure enough, around ten o'clock the following morning, Greyson called. But I was too disgusted with him at that time to even answer. He left a voicemail apologizing, saying he got caught up in a recording session at the studio and that his phone had died, so he couldn't call me. It sounded like a bunch of crap to me, so I didn't even bother to respond. He called and texted me several more times over the course of that weekend, but I had nothing to say to him. As far as I was concerned, I was done. Then at work that Monday, around lunchtime, I was paged to the front office. When I got up there, I couldn't believe my eyes.

Greyson had sent me the biggest and most beautiful floral arrangement that I had ever seen. It held three dozen red roses with a cute brown teddy bear holding a card that read, "I'm so sorry. Please give me another chance. Love, Greyson." I was completely floored.

Needless to say, I forgave him; the first of numerous times. Things have pretty much been that way ever since. Out of nowhere, Greyson will do or say something that really hurts my feelings or breaks my heart, or I'll "discover" some unscrupulous thing he's done. Then he'll go out of his way to apologize by doing something really big to mend it. I have a closet full of designer handbags and shoes, to diamond earrings and bracelets that are all "I'm sorry" gifts from Greyson. Granted, that's not entirely a bad thing, but it's not good either.

A lot has happened between Greyson and me over the years. He has certainly cheated; more than once. But when I tell you I love this man, I need you to understand that there's no limit to my love for him, and sometimes I hate myself for it.

I have done any and EVERYTHING to try to make Greyson happy and keep him satisfied. One time, I even let him stand in the bathtub and pee all over me! I still can't believe I did that, but it was something kinky he wanted to try, and I didn't want to tell him "no," because I knew some other "freakazoid" woman would very easily say "yes."

Over time, I've found other ways to deal with it all. First, I don't stress over what Greyson is doing or who he's doing it with. I mean, the thought of him out cheating with another woman still makes me sick, but it's not the thought of him having sex with her that bothers me so much. It's the thought of him spending time, sharing his secrets, and falling in love with her that tears me to pieces. I'm sure you probably won't agree, but as long as he's using protection, the physical act of him having sex with another woman isn't the worst thing in the world to me. Losing him is.

The second thing I do to help myself deal with my life as Mrs. Greyson (by the way, my husband's first name is Kevin, but I've always called him by his last name) is write songs. Greyson introduced me to the behind-the-scenes world of music when we first met, and I immediately took an interest in songwriting. Since then, he's let me work on a few mini projects over the years to help me perfect my craft.

Greyson made a home studio out of the third bedroom in our condominium a couple of years ago. He kind of trained me on the basics for recording a song. While I'm hardly the best singer in the world, I can hold a few notes, so I get in there from time to time to record songs that I've written. It's quite therapeutic. Outside of my students, it helps deal with the many peaks and valleys that make up my crazy ass life.

Listen, I'm not saying I condone infidelity, nor am I giving him a "pass" to cheat. But, a man is going to do what a man is going to do. Kicking, cussing, arguing, and making accusations every day isn't going to stop him from cheating, if that's what he *wants* to do. At worst or at best (depending on how you look at it), he'll just leave; or eventually, you will....

2

Greyson and I just had the most amazing, completely breathtaking, love session. He's over there knocked out right now, and snoring very loudly, as usual, so I don't even have to wonder if I did my part. But before tonight, it had been almost two weeks since we had sex. Well, since he and I had sex together. Lord, why am I even allowing my mind to go there? Tonight was a great night; well, for the most part. Let me just relish in that.

So, the evening started with dinner at McKendrick's. I love their steak. We ate well, had a few cocktails, and some really great conversation. I love how our date nights always make me feel like I did when we first started dating eight years ago. Greyson gave me updates on a few big projects he's working on. That always makes me feel good because he doesn't always keep me in the loop. All I know is when he's gone, at all times of the night, he's "working" or in a "session." And really, I don't truly know that for sure. Sometimes I have my doubts as to his whereabouts, but I try not to question him too much, even though I would be justified in doing so. Plus, he really, really hates it when I question him. He gets so defensive. I mean, loud and crazy defensive. The way he acts, you'd think he has this perfectly polished and immaculate track record. No Greyson, you have cheated on ME more times than I care to acknowledge. So, uh yeah, I may sometimes wonder if you really are where you say you are, actually doing what you tell me you're doing. Anyway, I digress.

As I was saying, since I can actually see the fruits of Greyson's labor, and benefit from them as well, I don't question his whereabouts too often. I just try to go with the flow and be the good wife that he enjoys coming home to at night; well, on the nights he actually comes home.

So back to tonight, after dinner, we popped into this trendy little lounge in Midtown. It had a nice mixed crowd, mostly with folks in their thirties like Greyson and me; a few older and some younger. They had these things called Hookahs. My husband finally convinced me to try one. I'm not a smoker, but I was feeling loose and somewhat I-don't-give-a-fuckish, so I went for it. In my opinion, it's not like smoking a cigarette or cigar, because it doesn't stink. It may have tobacco or nicotine in it; I can't say for sure. However, it's more like a vapor, a flavored liquid in fact. You smoke it from a hose that's attached to this big, curvy vase-like water bowl. And essentially, you're just inhaling the vapors from the liquid. That probably doesn't make it much healthier than a cigarette, but at least it isn't smoky. And if nothing else, it looks cool as shit. Plus, it gives you a slight buzz, or it'll enhance the one you already have; at least it did for me. It was fun.

I was already quite tipsy when we got to the hookah bar, but Grey got us more drinks anyway. We laughed, we danced, and really just got lost in enjoying ourselves, and each other's company. Best of all, Grey didn't pull out his phone the whole night! That never happens, but he promised me at the start of our evening, that he wouldn't. He wanted to make tonight all about me. He kept his word, at least for the most part.

After leaving the lounge around eleven o'clock, the night got even more interesting. Of course, at this point, we both were feeling no pain. The liquor was flowing freely inside of our bodies, and by this time, we were fired up! Greyson, being who he is, asked if I wanted to stop by Magic City to top off our evening. I had to catch myself before I responded with my first thought. Magic City is a popular strip club in Atlanta, Georgia. So, did I want to go? Not especially. But was I drunk? Absolutely. So, was I pretty much down for whatever? Indeed. With that, I gave Greyson the green light, and we made our way to the wonderful world of "tits-n-tails."

The parking lot was packed when we got there, so we immediately pulled up for valet. On our way there, I touched up my makeup, gave myself a couple of spritzes of Tory Burch, and unbuttoned the top buttons on my blouse. I felt like I needed to show a little more cleavage, what little I have, especially since we were about to be surrounded by nothing but beautiful, well-endowed, naked women. I didn't want to feel too plain.

As we made our way inside, I almost forgot that I needed to hide my eyes. Luckily, I had my favorite pair of Michael Kors sunglasses in my bag. They were cute, dark, and just what I needed because I wanted to feel disguised. Granted, I have been to the strip club with Greyson at least twenty times over the course of our relationship and marriage. Not once has it ever been my suggestion to go, but I usually have a good time when we do go. Plus, I know it's a turn-on for Grey. So, I do it for him more than anything. Now don't get me wrong, over time I've actually come to enjoy looking at the girls myself. I'm amazed at their bodies, and by the way, they can make parts of their body move while the rest of it stands still. I would be lying if I said it didn't arouse me sometimes. However, I am so not comfortable with looking a stripper in the eye. And I don't want anyone looking at me, while I'm looking at a stripper, in the eye. It makes me feel too "studdish;" like I'm a dude or something. Most importantly, I'm always worried that someone from school will recognize me. Maybe that shouldn't concern me because they'd have to be there themselves in order to see me, but it does.

I'm an elementary school teacher, a very dedicated one at that. I've won many awards and accolades over the course of my twelve-year career, so a lot of people know and respect me. They expect me to be poised, conservative, and a respectable woman at all times, because that's all I've ever shown them. Therefore, that's all they know, which isn't altogether a bad thing. In fact, I suppose it's a good thing since it says a lot about me and my character. But guess what? I'm human too. I'm not perfect, quite possibly the furthest thing from it. I think I've gotten so good at hiding the not-so-pretty sides of my life that most who know me, or at least think they do, believe I have a pretty perfect life and marriage. Boy, they are wrong. But for now, I'll let them continue believing that if they so choose. It's just funny to me how many people think I don't drink, party, or even "cuss," and not because I told them that I didn't, but because I never told them or showed them that I did. As far as I'm concerned, everyone doesn't need to know everything about me and my life. So yes, the sunglasses in the strip club are a must; the darker, the better. Thank goodness I had them tonight.

When we finally got inside the *city of magic*, Grey requested a table close to the stage. Then he gave me his bank card and sent me to the ATM inside the club to withdraw five hundred dollars. We swapped out most of the large bills for one dollar bills, so we could make it "rain," just a little bit, while in the building. Greyson knows I'll start giving him the side-eye if he starts spending more money than that in a booby bar, at least in my presence. Every now and then, I'll let him go a little crazy, but only on special occasions like his birthday.

We got our table and hadn't been seated for more than twenty seconds before we were bombarded by two "amazons," both with long wavy weaves flowing down to the tops of their big, juicy, possibly surgically enhanced, asses. With their super high heels on, each stood close to 5'10, if not taller. These were some healthy girls, but not fat or anything; just super-duper thick. They were almost a little intimidating as they towered over me.

I declined my red-haired vixen's offer for a lap dance. I needed a few more minutes to get situated and scope out the scenery. But Greyson insisted that they both dance for us. He's always doing the absolute most. So, there I was, seated, no drink in my hand, and this girl's freshly-waxed cookie staring me right in the face, and gyrating. My booze from earlier had already started to taper off, so I was feeling a little uncomfortable. I did not want to look at the dancer that up close and personal, not right away. I'm definitely not taking anything away from her, she was really very pretty, with a nice, deep-dimpled smile. I just needed a few more minutes and another drink ASAP.

Meanwhile, as I was still waiting for the waitress to deliver my *Miami Vice*, Greyson was on dance number four with the *same* dancer he started with. I was trying to play cool, as I always do, but it was starting to piss me off. He hadn't said one word to me since we sat down, and he never does that, because he knows how I need to "warm up" when we're in these kinds of establishments. Usually, we get a table and Greyson orders us drinks. Then we talk and joke around a little bit while checking out the girls and seeing what's what. If girls walk over right away, Greyson will just tell them to circle back with us in a few. But strangely tonight, he didn't do that.

The tall, curvy stripper was doing way more than just dancing for my husband. She was practically fucking him; right there, in the chair, across from me. Her breasts were huge, and she was rubbing her hard nipples all over his face. I even saw him hold his tongue out a few times to lick them. Yeah, he was tipsy, but that's no excuse. I should have stopped the show right then and there. At the very least, I should have said something or just flipped the whole damn table over. Regretfully, I didn't. I know, stupid, but let's not go there right now.

Anyhow, completely naked, with her long legs fully straddled across Grey's lap, the stripper, whose name I later learned was Blaze, was grinding and bouncing all over my husband's undoubtedly bulging and throbbing penis. It was like they were lost in their own world over there. I could not believe it. I was ready to walk out. Then my drink came.

The song that the DJ was playing when the waitress finally brought my drink over, came to an end. In the strip club world, that means patrons pay for another lap dance if they want a stripper to keep on dancing for them. In that instance, I said to myself, "If this negro pays for another dance from this girl, and still doesn't look over, to at least acknowledge me, I'm gone." And sure enough, he did. He told her to keep dancing, and he never gave me even half a glance.

Infuriated, but still trying to be a "lady" and not make a scene, I softly, but sternly, pushed my barely-touched drink over to his side of the table. I stood up, grabbed my purse, and headed for the door. I felt nauseous. I was really hoping that Grey would look up and notice my exit, that his wife was leaving, but he didn't. He was too engulfed in his slut-bucket dancer to even care.

When I got outside, the chilly fall air instantly hit me. I had no sweater or jacket, so I called for an Uber right away and prayed that it wouldn't take more than a few minutes to arrive. While waiting, one of the guys from security could see that I was upset. He'd actually seen more than I wish he had. So, in an attempt to comfort me, he said, "You're beautiful, don't let Blaze ruin your night." Before asking who the hell Blaze was, I gave him the ugliest look. Thinking, "Who the hell is he talking about?" Then he quickly clarified that for me, "Blaze, the dancer, the one that's been at y'all table since you got here. It's just entertainment baby. If you come to the strip club with your man, what do you expect him to do?" He chuckled. Just that quick, he had me pissed off even more. Why the hell was he all up in my business?

"Go back in there and have fun baby girl. You're a beautiful woman and Blaze ain't got nothing on you," the security guard continued. He was lying about her not having "nothing" on me, but I appreciated the compliment, and it did keep me from snapping at him by telling him to mind his own business. However, I knew I wasn't going back in there, not for anything. Right then, my phone went off. I thought it was my driver trying to reach me, but it was a text from Greyson, asking "Where are you?" I simply replied, "I'm gone, enjoy the rest of your night." A few seconds later, my Uber pulled up, and as I got in, I heard a voice shouting, "Noel! Noel!" It was Grey, but at this point, I was tired, I was hurt, and I didn't care. So, I didn't even look back. I slammed the door and asked the driver to pull off.

Immediately, Greyson started blowing up my phone. I wasn't about to put my business out there for the driver to hear, so after Grey called about ten times back to back, I just turned my phone off altogether.

On the way home, we ran into a little bit of traffic due to construction; the ride took a lot longer than it should have. This gave me a lot of time to think. I had to ask myself, "Why am I so in love and loyal to this man?" "Why do I let him get away with some of the bullshit he does?" I didn't have an answer for either question, other than, "Because I love him." However, I was glad I walked out tonight. I have never done that. I still didn't feel like I had won though. I knew what I had just done probably pissed Grey off tremendously, and that he would somehow turn the whole thing around on me and make it seem like I was the one who was wrong; like he always does. He'd probably use my storming out tonight as an excuse to go back inside the club, grab Blaze, and take her to the V.I.P. room. Then he'd pay her to suck his dick.

◊

What should have been no more than a twenty-minute ride, took about an hour. There's always some crazy road construction project going on in Atlanta that will have you tied up in traffic at the most unexpected times of day and night. It drives me crazy. Despite it, I was glad to be home. I just wanted to get inside my condo, take a shower, and go to bed.

It was a little after two o'clock in the morning when we pulled up in front of my building. I made my way through the lobby and realized I wasn't familiar with the Concierge who manages the front desk overnight, since I normally come in through the parking garage and bypass the lobby, so I stopped and introduced myself. Her name was Faith. Apparently, she's been working at our property location for about six months now and has already met Greyson. She seems really sweet, nice authentic personality; at least from what I gathered three minutes.

As I got on the elevator to make my way up to the eleventh floor, my stomach was in knots. I couldn't help but think about what Greyson was possibly doing at that very moment and whether or not he would even come home tonight. It made me mad, sad, and sick all at the same time. I couldn't help but wonder why I always had to deal with so much bullshit when it came to my husband. It's always something; always.

I fondled to get my house keys out of my purse as I got off of the elevator. I was relieved that I had even thrown them in my bag considering the night's turn of events. When I got inside, I immediately kicked off my heels. My feet were burning. I turned my phone back on and immediately a series of voicemails and texts from Grey chimed through. I wasn't in the mood to read or listen to them. I just wanted to take a hot shower and go to bed.

Before I hopped in the shower, I made sure it was good and hot. I opened Pandora on my phone and placed it on the counter, in hopes that a little music would help me relax. Once inside, the water from the oversized, rainfall shower head felt wonderful. We remolded our master bath a couple of months ago, and this was one thing I absolutely had to have. With my eyes closed, I felt like it was washing all my worries away. The only thing that was missing was my husband.

No sooner than having that thought, did I feel a hand suddenly and aggressively grab me from behind. I was terrified! Then a voice whispered in my ear, "Do you want me to fuck you up?" I exhaled a sigh of relief. It was Greyson. He had actually brought his ass home.

His body felt so good pressed against mine. His big, oversized arms cradled me as he pulled me in closer, the water now drenching us both from head to toe. I could still smell his Bleu De Chanel cologne. It was hypnotizing. I wasn't exactly sure what was about to happen next, but I hoped Grey wasn't still too mad at me for leaving the club the way I did, and then not answering his calls. Believe it or not, he's been known to throw a fit when he feels like he's been disrespected, especially by me. Things like hanging up the phone in his face or blatantly ignoring his calls, even when he's in the wrong, drive him all-out crazy.

Well, my concern dissolved when Greyson pulled my wet hair to the side and softly began planting kisses all over my neck. Then he apologized for being an asshole earlier in the evening. How could I not forgive him? I'm in love with this man, and after all, he came home; immediately. All I could do was turn around and reach up to wrap my arms around my husband's neck and kiss him with burning passion. I could taste the remanence of cognac on his lips and tongue as he picked me up to straddle him and take all ten inches of his heavenly girth.

We made love for a good hour and twenty-seven minutes, yes I glanced over at the clock when we made our way to the bed from the shower. That was more than enough time for me because every minute of it was really, really good. Greyson must have felt a little guilty because he licked and sucked every nook and cranny on my body tonight. He normally doesn't do all that. I mean he always eats the cookies, but not necessarily the whole cookie jar. He even sucked on my fingers and toes. I had to return the favor. I sucked, and even swallowed, which I only do maybe a few times a year (swallowing that is). I still haven't completely gotten used to the salty taste and thick consistency of Grey's sperm. Maybe I never will, or maybe he just needs to drink more water. I don't know, but I know it's what he likes; correction "oral service" is something he LOVES; but what man doesn't? In order to keep the side chicks away, it's a must for me. I have to be his "lady in the streets, and HIS freak in the sheets," so I pretend like I absolutely love doing it for him when I do it. What can I say, deserving or not, I'm trying to keep my husband.

In less than an hour and a half, Grey made me explode three times and I managed to pull two massive eruptions out of him. That's why he's sleeping so soundly right now. Too bad I can't have any kids because he or she would have undoubtedly been conceived tonight, if the timing were right.

◊

Damn, the last thing I need to do is go to bed with the "baby thing" in my brain. That's a very sensitive subject for me. Luckily, Greyson doesn't want to have any children. So that makes me feel a little better, and not like I'm less of a woman because I may never be able to give him a junior version of himself or a sweet-pie-face princess. However, he did say if he ever changes his mind, we can always look into adopting a little one. But that's just another detail of my life that I keep to myself. Whenever a co-worker or acquaintance asks, "So when are you and the hubby going to start a family?" my well-rehearsed response is always, "Not just yet. Grey and I want to travel a little more before we officially put our lives on lockdown." I usually follow it up with a soft chortle, to make it believable. Then I have to fight back the tears.

The truth is, I'm infertile. I can't have kids. And the reason I can't have kids is because a trusted family member introduced me to the life of prostitution or escorting when I was a teenager. She would set me up with all kinds of men, including other family members. They would pay her two hundred dollars to have an hour with me, to do whatever they wanted to do, behind closed doors. Most of the time I received half of the money, sometimes a little more, to keep me quiet. I can't even begin to tell you all that was done to me. I was fingered, choked, spanked, spit on, and brutally fucked in just about every hole, even my navel. It was terrible. I was also on birth control, so half the time the men wouldn't wear condoms. They'd just cum inside of me. Mind you, these were married men, business men, but most of all, dirty-trifling-grimy men.

Ultimately, all that gross wear and tear on my body led me to be diagnosed with pelvic inflammatory disease, at seventeen years old. It was due to a sexually transmitted infection that was left untreated for too long. Sadly, it caused permanent damage to my reproductive organs, specifically my uterus and fallopian tubes. Therefore, it would take some sort of strange miracle, not only for me to conceive a child, but also for me to be able to carry him or her, even remotely close to full term.

Needless to say, I'm not volunteering those details up to anybody. I'm very selective in what I share with people, even my closest friend Nicole, my one *true* friend really, doesn't know half of the things going on in my life and marriage right now. Also, I'm sure she has no idea how badly I wish I could be a mommy like her, and that I secretly envy her because she is. That's why I haven't called her in a while. Still, she does know quite a bit about me, more than anybody in fact, even Greyson.

I'm just a private person I guess, and I may have some trust issues as well; understandably so. However, I just feel like the less people know about you, the less opportunity they have to use certain truths against you. I mean, why invite people in where they don't belong? I certainly don't want or need any of my not-so-pretty business exposed. It would only make life harder. I'd always feel like I had to explain myself or my life choices to others.

And I don't have time for that. Life is hard enough by itself.

With that said, despite what most might believe, because of the impression I've given them, my life is definitely not perfect, nor am I, nor is my husband. And that's okay because we're going to be okay regardless. I believe that with my whole heart. So, I don't need any input or second opinions from anyone who isn't in this bedroom, right here, right now.

Yes, I probably shouldn't have been so quick to move past Greyson's little stunt tonight, but guess what? It's my marriage. He's my husband. That makes it my business, and just another thing I'll have to keep to myself, to keep all the gossipy chatter at bay. When it boils down to it, I'll always find a way to press through whatever life or Greyson sends my way; good or bad. It's what I've always had to do.

Therefore, it's what I've always done. No doubt about it, I'm a loving, outgoing, and very vocal teacher when it comes to my students. But to the contrary, I'm a private, discreet introvert when it comes to my personal life. It is what it is.

Most of all, I just pray that Greyson gets it together and cuts out all the foolishness. I really want us to stay, and be happily married *forever*. I don't ever want to see the day where I *have to unlove* him. That's something I can't even begin to imagine. So, for now, I guess I'll have to be content, being his "number one." That'll make a good song.

3

I think I've cried every single hour of the day today. It's four o'clock in the afternoon now, and I've been up since five. So needless to say, there's been a whole lot of crying going on. I had to convince my very concerned first-grade class that Mrs. Greyson was just dealing with really bad allergies today. They offered to sing me songs and a few even colored up "get well" cards for me, all in hopes that it would make me feel better. It did. They're the absolute sweetest. That's why I go all out for them. I reward them with a "*Pizza & Fresh Fruit Friday*" at least twice a month; all happily funded by me. I look forward to seeing their little snaggletooth faces every day. They're my sunshine.

◊

You'd think that after twenty years, it would get easier, but I can't say that it has. One thing about moms, they can't ever be replaced; ever. I guess time does help with the healing process, but the void in your heart is never completely filled, and the hurt never completely goes away. My mom died when I was thirteen years old. Today would have been her 50th birthday, and I miss her just as much today, as I did on the day she left this earth.

Greta was beautiful. I loved everything about her. To me, she was perfect. I was an only child. Well, I was my mother's only child. I can't say the same about my dad. He left us when I was six years old, and I haven't heard from him since; not a letter, not a phone call, not one birthday card, nothing, in twenty-seven years. For a long time, it hurt me to my very core. I cried like crazy. That pain only intensified after my mother passed away.

Unbelievably, when my mom was alive, she never spoke bad about my dad for doing what he did to us, at least not to me. When I'd ask, "Why did he leave?" or "When is daddy coming back?" my mom's only reply, each and every time, would be, "Daddy just found happiness somewhere else sweetie. One thing about men, you can't make'em stay. And we're not gonna' worry about it, cause you know what? Life goes on." I'm sure her heart broke a little more each time she had to tell me that.

Life did go on for us, but it was hard; especially at first. When my dad left, the mortgage on the house was several months behind. My mom did the best she could to get it caught up and keep it caught up. She worked at a distribution warehouse for a big snack company during the day. Then she picked up a second job at a local grocery store, and worked part-time at night. Needless to say, if nothing else, we always had food in the house.

Back when my mom and dad first got married, we moved to Atlanta by way of Chicago. We didn't have any family down here, so when my dad left, my mother's options for child care were very limited. She certainly didn't have the money to pay for it. Therefore, while my mom worked, I spent most of my time either home alone or at our neighbor's house, Ms. Kimberly. She had a daughter who was close to my age. Her name was Nicole. We clicked immediately. We don't talk or see each other as often as we should, but to this day, she's still my best friend.

◊

From a very early age, I recognized how hard my mom worked to keep a roof over our heads. I understood her sacrifice, and I appreciated her for it. She went out her way to create meaningful memories with me. We'd always cook together, have picnics in the park, or spend Saturdays baking cookies and flipping through the big, thick JC Penny's catalogs and other home & fashion magazines, turning down the corners of the pages, marking the things we were going to buy ourselves when we were finally "rich."

Well, we never became rich, at least not in my mom's lifetime. In fact, we ended up losing our car and our house, about a few months after my mom got laid off from her job at the snack company. I'll never forget looking outside of my bedroom window one night. Mom had just thrown me a really nice party earlier that day, for my thirteenth birthday. We invited a few girls from my school, but mostly kids from the neighborhood. Mom went all out, even hired a DJ. And although I'm certain she couldn't afford it, she bought me a beautiful sterling silver and opal pendant necklace, with earrings to match. I still have it to this day.

Anyway, I looked outside my window, just as I was heading to bed and I saw something that absolutely terrified me. Two men were stealing our car! I ran to my mother's room to wake her and let her know what was happening. She quickly threw on her robe and ran out of the front door to confront the men. Then, from the front doorway, because she told me to stay in the house, I could hear her begging and pleading with the men not to take our car. I was a bit confused though. Since when did car thieves hang around to negotiate, with clipboards in their hands at that? Well, after giving her the opportunity to remove her personal belongings, and voluntarily turn over the car keys, my mom's car was repossessed.

That night, my mom cried her eyes out. She explained to me what has just happened. It hurt me so bad to see her like that because I knew how hard she worked. But even with swollen, tear-beaten eyes, she hugged me and told me, "Everything will be okay." I believed her. I really did.

I'm assuming it was shortly after my mom received the final letter, confirming the details of the foreclosure proceedings on our home that she decided to let me know that we would be moving soon. She expressed to me that she had done all that she could to keep it from happening, but it was happening, and we would have to leave. Although she still her job at the grocery store, now full-time, it was hardly enough to keep us afloat.

Around that time, my mom had lost a considerable amount of weight. I assumed it was because she had been eating less. However, one thing I knew for sure, she had been drinking a lot more. We didn't cook together as much anymore either. Instead, mom would come home, ask about my day, and listen half-heartedly as she poured herself a glass of wine or some other brown liquor. Then she'd retreat to her bedroom, close the door, and spend the rest of the evening listening to sad love songs on her record player and smoking Black & Mild cigars; only popping out occasionally to top off her glass.

◊

Weeks passed, and my mom still hadn't told me where we'd be moving. She hadn't even brought one single box in the house for us to pack. Then, one Thursday, I was paged to the front office at school, just as I was getting my lunch tray. I thought it was odd and I immediately knew something was wrong.

When I got to the front office, I instantly noticed Ms. Kimberly standing near the doorway, blanketed in tears. My heart dropped. I knew something had happened to my mom. Before Ms. Kimberly or my school counselor could even finish their sentence to tell me that my one and only mother, my heart, my best friend, my EVERYTHING, was dead, I passed out.

I woke up laying on a bed inside the school nurse's office. Ms. Kimberly was still there, standing over me and holding my hand. I really wanted to believe it was all just a bad dream. But it wasn't. My mom was gone, and she wasn't coming back.

I later learned that we were being evicted from our home that day, something my mom already knew, but didn't share with me. When the eviction guys arrived to remove all of our belongings from the house, they found my mom in her bed, unconscious. On her stomach were three white envelopes; one addressed to me, one to Ms. Kimberly, and one addressed to the "Eviction Guys." Next to the bed was a bottle of prescription pain pills and a bottle of over-the-counter sleeping pills; she had killed herself.

What made the worst day of my life, even worse, was knowing that my mom "chose" to leave me. She was all I had. And though it took a long while, as I've gotten older, I've grown to forgive her. Having experienced so many peaks and valleys in my lifetime, I think I can relate to the pain and sense of hopelessness that my mom felt on the day she decided to end her own life. But what has kept me, aside from God's grace, are the last words my mom left for me in that white envelope:

My Sweet Birdy,

If you're reading this letter right now, I know your heart is probably very broken and I am so sorry. This goes against everything I've ever taught you. I know you may never understand why things had to end up this way. Honestly, I don't either. However, I want you to promise me that you'll keep believing in God and never give up on yourself or on life, no matter what comes your way, and despite what I have done. There's just a lot going on in my head and in my heart that you're too young to understand. But please know that I tried to be the very best mom that I could be for you and I never, ever wanted to leave you this way. I love you so much and just want the very best for you. And I think this is for the best.

I'm leaving a letter for Ms. Kimberly, that tells her what to do in order to collect the money from my life insurance policy. This will help take care of you and pay for you to go to college when it's time. Hopefully, you'll be able to live with them until then.

Well my lil Birdy, I guess this is goodbye for now. But we'll see each other again. I promise. And remember, just cause you think it's over, really it isn't over. Life goes on. And you will get pass the bad days. Troubles may come but won't stay. Cause life goes on... I love you Noel and I'm so sorry. I'll always be watching over you. So please forgive me, be strong for mommy, and no matter what, don't ever give up.

Love always,

Mommy

I really wish my mom had taken her own advice, and just held on. However, being a thirty-three-year-old woman, who's lived through some real things, I've had moments where I prayed for death to come and find me. Because of that, part of me understands why my mom did what she did; right or wrong. Granted, I still don't believe it was the right or the best thing to do for either one of us. It certainly doesn't make my heart hurt any less when I think about her. I'd give ANYTHING in the world to have my beautiful Greta back; anything. I miss that sweet lady so much. Can't wait to see her again….

4

I'm staying in a hotel tonight. Actually, this will be the second night in a row. I didn't go in to work today either, and I doubt that I'll make it in tomorrow. My babies will probably bombard their substitute teacher with all kinds of questions regarding my whereabouts if they haven't done so already, but especially if I'm *M.I.A.* two days in a row. After all, a couple of months ago, I did spend an entire day openly grieving in front of them, on my late mother's birthday. So I can understand any concern they might have. I tell you, to be so young, my students are wise beyond their years. Kids these days know and understand far more things about life, and even love than we give them credit. My little first grade boogers really adore me, and I love them more than they'll ever know. So, I really should pull myself together and show up for class tomorrow. But, I don't think I can do it. Right now, my soul is completely crushed. I could just die….

Good or bad, we all have at least a few significant days or moments in our lives that we'll never forget. You know the ones where you can always recall what you were wearing or what you were eating, or even what scent was in the air at the time. Well, this past Tuesday was one of those days for me. And I'll never ever forget it, not for as long as I live.

Earlier this year, Greyson committed to shutting everything down at his recording studio by six o'clock, at least one day a week. He did this because he was tired of hearing me complain about us not spending enough time together. Grey gives a whole new meaning to being a "workaholic." With all sides of his music business booming right now, it seems like I've been placed on the back burner increasingly more these days. So, out of an effort to make me happy, but more so to shut me up, he agreed to make it home in time for dinner, at least once a week. For the most part, he kept his commitment, usually on Tuesdays.

This week, Grey wanted to switch it up from our usual Taco Tuesday menu. I agreed it would be good to do something different, even though I love Mexican food. I could eat it almost every day. However, we decided to go with Chinese food. Well, Grey decided that. Since I'm not one hundred percent sure that the Chinese take-out "chicken" is actually chicken, and not skinned cats or mice packaged to look like chicken, (I've read some horror stories) I opted to cook dinner myself. I've gotten pretty good at whipping up Grey's favorites; General Tso's chicken, shrimp fried rice, and egg rolls. If I could master a good recipe for Hot & Sour soup, I'd probably never step foot in a Chinese restaurant again.

When I got off work on Tuesday, I headed to the grocery store to get the things I needed for dinner. I picked up two bottles of wine; one for me to pop open and start enjoying while I prepared dinner and the other was primarily for Greyson. While I was shopping, he called to check on me and also to warn me to be prepared to have my "back banged out" later that evening. It made me blush. He had been sending me flirty, erotic, and down-right-nasty text messages all day. It was clear he needed some "action" and I was going to be ready to give it to him when he got home; hence the wine.

After trudging my way through traffic from Decatur to Buckhead, I managed to make it home a little after five. I figured Grey would make it home close to seven, since that's about the time he normally arrives. That gave me just enough time to shower, get comfy, and cook.

◊

I was in a great mood. Before I got dinner started, I lit one of my favorite candles, turned on some music, and poured myself a chilled glass of Riesling. The candle smelled amazing, Jo Malone Pomegranate, which was an unusually more expensive gift from one of my students.

As I was preparing the fried rice for dinner, I realized we were low on soy sauce. I called Grey to ask him to pick up some, but he didn't answer, so I left him a message. About forty-five minutes went by and I still hadn't heard back from Grey. By this time, it was after seven. I didn't bother to call him again because I assumed he would be walking through the door at any given minute. Instead, I decided to pour myself another glass of wine and sit back and relax.

Before I could make my way to the living room, to plop down on the sofa, I snuck in a big bite of my home-made chicken fried rice. Right then, my phone rang. It was Greyson. I answered it, but I couldn't speak right away because my mouth was full. I quickly put the phone on speaker, as I gulped down the food in my mouth. That's when I heard a voice on the other end of the phone, but it wasn't Greyson's.

It was a woman's voice on the other end, and I heard her ask, very seductively, "You like that baby?" Then I heard Greyson's trifling ass moan and reply, "You know I do. Put all that dick in your mouth. Don't stop." After that, I could clearly hear the sound of this bitch sucking and slobbin' all over my piece-of-shit-ass husband's dick and him moaning and grunting like it was the best head he ever had in his life. Clearly his pants were around his ankles, and somehow he managed to pocket dial me in the mist of this scandalous bullshit.

I could not fuckin' believe what I was hearing. My heart sank, and my stomach was completely in knots, but I couldn't stop listening. I wanted to hear it all. So I put the phone on mute, braced myself, and just listened.

I sat there at the breakfast bar, in the middle of my kitchen for over an hour, and listened to my husband fuck the shit out of another woman. I only got up to pour myself another glass of wine and then to open the other bottle, which I ended up finishing as well. I heard them as they made their way to bed, and then as she climbed on top to ride him. They were flirting, laughing, and talking really raunchy to each other the entire time. I heard him as he told her to bend over so he could "hit that fat ass from the back" and as her ass slapped very loudly with each thrust of his dick. I heard him smacking his lips as he ate her out, telling her how good she tastes. I even heard him tell her that she had the best pussy he ever had, how good it smelled, and that any man would be a fool to let her go. Okay, that's when I cried.

It hurt me so bad. Greyson has done a lot of things, but this was an all-time low. He knew I was at home preparing dinner for us to enjoy together. He knew I was waiting. But he didn't care. Instead, he chose to spend the evening with another woman and didn't even pay me the due diligence of calling and lying to me, ahead of time, claiming he would be late or wasn't coming home right away because he got tied up with something really important at work that couldn't wait. And I guess he wouldn't have been lying had he told me that. Judging by his actions that night, and by the "sounds" of it alone, that homewrecker was really important to him, more important than me, and apparently, she couldn't wait.

Just when I thought the moment couldn't cut me any deeper, it did. As I continued eavesdropping, I could tell Greyson was about to cum. The tremble in his voice, as he continued to talk dirty to her, and the increasingly harder and faster sound of his body pounding against hers were dead giveaways. It was in those seconds that Greyson's words violently snatched all the breath from my body, sending me plummeting to the floor.

"I can't let you go," he told her, still fucking her and barely able to speak at this point. Then he asked her, "You sure wanna have my baby, cause I'm bout to cum all up in this pussy." She said, "Yes, daddy." Then he came.

I couldn't hold it in. I immediately began throwing up all over the kitchen floor. There was so much of it. It came up and out with such great force that I peed on myself. Too weak to move, I laid there for at least ten minutes, right there in my own vomit and urine.

The phone was still on mute, so I could still hear Greyson. His voice suddenly got closer and then there was a scuffling noise. It was going on ten o'clock, and finally, Grey decided to dig his phone out of his pants pocket, and perhaps, give me a call. I think that's when he realized that I was already on the line.

I heard him whisper, "Oh shit." Then the call disconnected.

◊

I was drunk, I was hurt, and I was infuriated. I had no words for Greyson, and I certainly didn't want to be home when he got there. I knew it wouldn't go well. But before I could clean myself up and pack an overnight bag, my mind completely snapped! There was no way I was going to let Grey get away with this bullshit, not this time. He had gone too far, and I had heard too much.

Before I knew it, I had filled our oversized bathtub with water, but I didn't get in it. Instead, I went inside our home recording studio and took every piece of equipment that would fit, and dumped it over into the tub. I didn't care what it was or how much it cost. It was gone, including his Mac Books that contained a lot of his music files.

Then I began to panic. As angry as I was, I knew it would pale in comparison to what Greyson would feel once he discovered what I had done out of retaliation. He would probably try to kill me. There was no way I could have been there when he arrived; that I knew for sure.

I hastily changed my clothes, didn't even bother to shower. I threw some clothes and shoes in an overnight bag. Then I grabbed my keys, phone, and purse and raced out of the door. I didn't even bother to lock it. My bodily fluids still covered the kitchen floor.

My heart was pounding so fast, as I prayed not to run into Greyson on my way out. I was too afraid to take the elevator to the parking garage, fearing the door would open and Grey would be standing right there, plus I knew I smelled awful. So I took the stairs.

I managed to make it to my car without running into Grey or anyone else I knew from the building. But right as I was pulling out of the parking garage, I saw Greyson making his way up the drive to pull in. It was dark, but I was certain he would recognize our Range Rover as we passed each other. I could feel my chest tighten up because just as I thought, he did.

Luckily, the windows are deeply tinted on the truck. So, when Grey stopped his car and rolled down his window to get my attention, I just acted like I didn't see him. Then I sped out of the parking lot. When I got up a few blocks, I checked my review mirror to make sure he wasn't following me. After about thirty minutes, he started blowing up my phone with both texts and calls. I assumed by then he discovered the damage I'd left behind, so anything he had to say at that point was likely very threatening. I didn't need to hear it. By this time, I knew I wouldn't be showing up for class on Wednesday. I also knew I wouldn't be getting any rest either.

After a couple of hours, Grey had stopped ringing my phone. I still hadn't read any of his messages or listened to any of his voicemails. I was still crying profusely. By then, I no longer cared if Greyson was mad at me. I didn't even care if he wanted to kill me. I felt like he already had.

◊

It's Thursday and Grey and I still haven't spoken, at least not verbally. I finally got around to reading his texts and listening to his voicemails, and surprisingly, not one of them was threatening in any way. He expressed his initial disgust at what I had done to his equipment, but he didn't pretend like he didn't know the reason why I had done it. He didn't call me out my name or anything. He only apologized, over and over again and asked me to call him so we could talk. When he hadn't gotten any response from me by Wednesday afternoon, he started blowing my phone up again. He begged me to just text him and let him know I was ok. So I did that. But that's it, nothing more and nothing less.

Really, I don't know how to move forward from all of this. Like this has really broken my heart into a million pieces. I've forgiven my husband for a lot of shit, but I don't think I can this time. I just feel so betrayed. This is way bigger than him fucking another woman. He's actually planning a family with her!

I'm heartbroken beyond words, but I can't be mad at Grey for wanting to have a child of his own; even if I can't give it to him. Yes, my life has been shitty. Yes, I lost my mom to suicide when I was thirteen years old. Yes, I was forced to go live with my shit hole aunt, who was only out to collect the money from my mom's life insurance policy. Yes, she started pimping me out to men when I was fourteen years old when the life insurance money ran out. Yes, that was such a fucked-up thing to do! And yes, as a result, I can't have kids now. But no, it's not my fault, and no, it's not Greyson's either.

Greyson knows a lot of the particulars from my very storied past, even if he doesn't know everything, and he still chose to marry me anyway. That means a lot to me. I know there are always women clamoring for him and his attention, and maybe his money now, but he chose me. That was something he didn't have to do. I'm always reminded of that during times like this, even if this proves to be the final breaking point.

I really wish my mom were here right now. But I'm not sure what she would say. Maybe she'd remind me that I can't keep a man that doesn't want to be kept. So if Greyson has found happiness somewhere else, like my dad did when I was a little girl, then I'll just have to let him go like my mom did; no matter how much I love him. Of course, the very thought of Grey being happy with someone else, or even happier, completely shreds me. However, I have been the best wife that I know how to be, and if I'm still not good enough, then I'm just not good enough. I can't make him stay. I wouldn't even want him to.

◊

Knowing what I know now, how do I get past this? What if this girl is pregnant? What the fuck am I supposed to do with that, help them raise their child? It's such a fucking slap in the face, but in all of Grey's messages, he's been insisting that we need to talk, insisting she doesn't mean anything to him. Of course, he doesn't know what all I actually heard, but he knows it was enough; more than enough.

I'm not sure how all of this is going to end. Honestly, it hurts too much to even think about it. It could go so many ways, and most of those ways don't favor me. Hell, none of it favors me. Yet, I do know, one way or another, I must get past this. I will get past this. It's a horrible situation to be in, but I've been through worse. Even though it feels like it right now, I know it's not the end of the world. It can't be.

Mom must be here with me right now because suddenly I started feeling like I'll survive this. I know it won't be easy and I know I'm not done crying. I probably won't ever be done crying. Even still, I'm not ready to talk to Grey just yet. I'm not sure what he has to say anyway. He could tell me that he wants to leave. And although I accept that as being a possibility, and that it might be for best for the both of us, it still isn't news I'm racing to hear.

For now, I'm just going to focus on pulling myself together enough to make it to school tomorrow. I miss my babies. I may even stop and pick up some donuts and orange juice for them on my way in. They'll love that. I need to see them and feel their energy, my drops of sunshine. They always remind me that no matter what, life goes on.

5

I'm convinced that I'm being punished for something. That has to be it. I'll admit it, I haven't lived a perfect life, but that's primarily because I haven't had a perfect life. It's been one dreadful event after another. It all started when dad left mom and me to fend for ourselves when I was six years old. My heart has never fully recovered from that. Had he stayed, I know my life would have been a lot sweeter, and just better because my mom would still be alive, and here with me.

Though we had our share of struggles, mom and I had a lot of happy times together. Things never really seemed that bad to me. Maybe it was because Greta just knew how to make the most out of everything. But then again, I was a kid, so she didn't let me know everything that was going on either. Sometimes I wish she had, though. Part of me feels like I could have saved her.

Once mom passed away, it was all downhill from there. I remember when my Aunt Jess showed up for her funeral. I was both shocked and disgusted to see her. She was my mom's only sister, out of four siblings. They never spoke much. My mom practically hated her. Even though I was a child, mom made it her business to let me know that Aunt Jess was just "*plain ol' trifling.*" She used to steal from my mom, lie on her, and one time she cut all of my mother's hair off while she was sleeping. Mom even walked in on her sucking my dad's wonky one time, just weeks after I was born. She slipped up and told me that one night after she had been drinking.

At thirteen years old, I knew there was a suspect reason my Aunt Jess flew down to attend my mom's home-going, and it wasn't because she loved her. None of my uncles made it. They were all broke deadbeats, who couldn't afford the plane ticket from Chicago.

I remember her trying to console me after the funeral, but her energy just felt cold and evil, so I stayed as close to Ms. Kimberly and Nicole as possible. I'm not sure what happened because I was all set to move into my bestie's house and live with her and her family. It was actually a highlight for me, under the extremely miserable circumstances. Then my Aunt Jess and Ms. Kimberly pulled me to the side to let me know that I would be flying back to Chicago to live with my aunt. I was devastated.

Somehow it was decided that it would be best for me to move back to Chicago to be with my family on my mother's side since my father nor any of my family on his side could be reached. I wanted to die. I knew it was going to be bad. But I couldn't have guessed, not in a million years, that it would have been as bad as it turned out to be.

Needless to say, my aunt's mission was accomplished. She became my legal guardian and was able to collect the money from my mom's life insurance policy, all of it. I'm not exactly sure how much it was, but I know she blew through it. It was all gone after about a year.

◊

For my fourteenth birthday, Jess threw me a surprise party/cookout at her apartment. What was immediately odd, was that she didn't have any other kids there, except an attending neighbor's two-year-old son. Jess claimed she was just trying to keep it simple since our place wasn't that big. It made sense. I guess.

I'd say we had about twenty folks crammed into the two-bedroom apartment. She invited my uncles, a few neighbors from the apartment complex, and some of her friends. Majority of the guests were men.

The grill was going out on the patio. The music was really loud. And the air was filled with weed and cigarette smoke. Everyone seemed to be having a good time, but not me. I remember making my way to the kitchen because I was getting hungry and hoped some of the food was ready. When I got in there, I saw my aunt making a big bowl of punch. She poured in a big can of Hawaiian Punch, then a bottle of pineapple juice followed up with a huge bottle of McCormick's vodka. Then she told me to grab a cup.

I was hesitant, but she insisted. She said I needed to relax and have fun since it was my fourteenth birthday and that I wasn't a little girl anymore.

About an hour later, I was standing on top of the cocktail table in the living room, dancing very provocatively; being egged on by everyone in the room. I had no business up there, popping and shaking to one of Luke's songs. But I was up there, and I was having a good time. Only fourteen, in a room full of grown ass men. And I was drunk.

I can't recall if I had two drinks or three, but I do know it wasn't long before I started feeling a little nauseous. My aunt told me I would be fine and just needed to go lay down. So I did. When I got to my room and sat on my bed, the room started spinning immediately. I couldn't lay back because it made me feel even woozier, so I just crouched over and held my head. Then I heard a soft tap at my door. Music was still blaring in the background, and I was too nauseated to speak loud enough, to tell whomever it was to come in.

Before I knew it, I was staring down at a pair of dingy, white run-down Nike's. The raggedy shoes belonged to Tony; he was one of our neighbors. He said my aunt had sent him to check on me. He was smoking a cigarette. I asked him if he could put it out because the smell of it was making me feel worse. He honored my request and stepped out of the room to put it out somewhere. I didn't expect him to come back, hoped he wouldn't. But he returned, and then I heard him lock the door.

Things got foggy after that, but I do know that Tony came and sat next to me on the bed and started rubbing my back. He told me I would be ok and that I just needed to lay down and get some rest. Next thing I knew, I was in the bed with my pants and panties off, and Tony was in between my legs licking away. I tried to push his head back, but he just pried my legs open even harder and told me to relax. After that, I think I passed out. But I do remember him climbing on top of me and forcing his dick inside of me. I also remember that it hurt like hell.

◊

When I woke up the next morning, I had blood spots all over my sheets, and my pom-pom was quite sore. At first, I was a little discombobulated. Then it all came back to me. I couldn't believe I had lost my virginity, and to Tony at that! Tony was nineteen years old and didn't have the best reputation; clearly. He wasn't very attractive either. His teeth were really crooked. He may have even been missing one or two of them in the front. He just looked bad. He smelled bad most of the time too; musty and fishy. Yuck!

I was so repulsed and scared. Even bigger, I didn't want my aunt to find out. I didn't want anybody to find out for that matter. So I quickly gathered up my soiled sheets to hide them, until I could find a way to wash them secretly. That's when I noticed two twenty-dollar bills laying on my nightstand. I had no idea where they came from, but assumed maybe my aunt left it for me as a birthday gift. I never asked her about it though, and she never mentioned it. In fact, she never mentioned anything about that entire night.

When I first made my way out of my bedroom that morning, I was so nervous that Jess would confront me about what happened in my bedroom the night before, between Tony and me. But she didn't. In fact, she wasn't even home. That was uncommon for her. I was relieved. I wanted to avoid her at all costs. When she did finally make it home later that day, she never brought it up. So, neither did I.

Words can't express how dirty I felt that morning, and for the many weeks and months that followed. It seemed like I could never wash Tony's musty, sweaty body odor off me. It was sickening. Eventually, I learned that he was the one who left the money for me. I had run into him a few weeks later while checking the mail and he asked if I needed any money. Unfortunately, at the time, I did. That moment opened up a gateway to hell for me; filled with sex, drugs, alcohol, and prostitution. Worst of all, it was all spearheaded by my Aunt Jess.

◊

I look back on that time in my life, and I cringe. It was really, really bad; totally and completely out of control. The crazy thing is, I absolutely hated all the crazy shit Jess had me doing at first, but then I started to like it. At that point, I knew my life was superiorly fucked up, so I felt I had nothing to lose. More importantly, I liked the money. I needed it.

After Jess ran through all the money that was supposed to be reserved for me, she made it a point to let me know I would have to make my own way, in order to survive. So I had to do something. However, that wasn't my only motivation. I also liked all the nice clothes and shoes I got to wear to school because I was making between $500-$800 a week after my aunt got her cut. I liked the sense of control that taking hard-earned money from men because they wanted to have sex with me, gave me. Jess would remind me that it was something most girls were doing for free anyway, might as well get paid for it.

She had me convinced that we were some sort of "dream team." When really, she was just "pimping" me.

◊

Heaven knows I have prayed and asked the Lord to forgive me for all of my sins, probably a million times, especially my sins from back then. I remember I'd sometimes get on my knees to pray and ask God to forgive me, right before I "turned a trick." Each time I also asked him to save me from doing it or somehow stop me from doing it, if I wasn't supposed to be doing it. But with my aunt always in my ear, telling me I had to do it because it was how we paid our bills, it was three years before a burning infection inside my private parts, brought it all to an end.

I'm sure I probably slept with a lot of married men, but I was young. I didn't know any better. Plus, the men never volunteered that information. I just recall seeing many of them wearing wedding bands. Jess told me to never inquire about their marital or relationship status because it was none of my business. I was there to do a job, and that's it. But I can't help but wonder if all that I'm going through with my marriage has anything to do with *karma,* from what I did back then. It's possible.

Although I'm not the most religious person, I do believe in God. But sometimes it's hard to. So much messed up shit has happened to me. It just doesn't seem fair. Regardless, I know he's up there and my mom's right beside him, watching over me. I hope mom isn't too heartbroken by some of the things she's seen. I hope she's proud of me for how far I've come and for what I have accomplished in life. I just pray that despite what I've done in the past, God forgives me. I hope he understands that I'm only human. I really try my best to be a good person, a great teacher, and an even better wife. Sometimes I fall short though. So, where I am dirty, may I be made *clean*... Amen.

6

Who knew so much could happen in six months. I certainly didn't. But Greyson has a baby on the way. And it's a girl. He and Blaze (the stripper) are really excited. I'm happy for them.

Bullshit, I hate them both! They have ruined my fucking life. I've had to start taking anxiety pills just to function every day, without losing my mind. I felt myself coming close to it though. It was really starting to feel like the whole world was caving in on me. Then, when I stopped by the drugstore on my way home from work one afternoon and purchased two bottles of sleeping pills, that was my clue to seek help. Thankfully, I didn't go home and take the pills, as I had contemplated. But that's when I knew I had to do something. If not, someone may have been delivering some heartbreaking news to my precious first grade class. I couldn't let that happen.

Unfortunately, I don't know how much longer I can stay on this medicine. It just makes me feel more tired than anything and kind of dazed. I don't like it. I have to have tons of energy to keep up with my students, and lately, I've been slacking. Plus, I still feel really sad and heartbroken, so the pills haven't helped too much with that. However, I don't feel like jumping off a bridge anymore or killing Greyson for that matter, at least not today. So that's a good thing.

I have to laugh to keep myself from crying because my life is twisted beyond comprehension right now. How in the hell did I end up here? Oh yea, my dad abruptly exited my life when I was a little girl. As a result, my judgment regarding men has been forever impaired. So yes, it's that bastard's fault.

Would you believe that I'm still with Grey's out-of-wedlock-baby-making ass, even after this confirmed news? It just doesn't stop. All that he is doing to prepare for his little girl's arrival is a slap in the face every day. Most days, I don't understand how I'm even still standing. However, I had the option to leave or stay, and I chose to stay. I chose to forgive my husband (again), for the whole fiasco that took place months back. You know the one that drove me to drown all of his expensive studio equipment in a tub of hot water? Still, to my defense, I decided to stay, before I knew he was *actually* having a baby with this other woman. I thought he just had sex with her. That was enough!

◊

After staying in a hotel for a week and avoiding just about all of my husband's attempts to communicate with me, I finally agreed to sit down and have a talk with him. I wasn't ready to come home yet, and I certainly wasn't letting him come to the hotel. So we agreed to meet at a shopping plaza, not too far from the condo. We sat inside of my truck and hashed things out. Ultimately, Grey served me up a big bowl of bullshit, with a cherry on top.

During our conversation, Grey must have apologized a hundred times, but it wasn't well received. The problem was that he wasn't clear on what he was apologizing for exactly. He certainly wasn't confessing anything. He just kept saying, "Baby I'm so sorry if I did anything to hurt you. Please forgive me. Please give me another chance." Then he went on to talk about how much I meant to him and how he never wanted to do anything to hurt me. I just wanted to punch him in his face! He was so full of shit.

Finally, I couldn't take it anymore, so I just told him to shut up. That's when I took the opportunity to let him know *everything* I had heard that crushing night when I was on the other end of the phone. The lump in his throat was very visible following that. But he knew he had to say something. He sat silently for a few moments at first and just stared out through the window. Somehow, he even managed to muster up a few tears. I was so over the dramatic scene he was trying to create, starring himself as the victim. It sent my last nerve into a tailspin. I went off on him and demanded that he tell me something, and it needed to be the truth. After that, he laid it all out.

First, he told me that the girl meant absolutely nothing to him. She was just a freak and something to fuck. I asked him where he met her. He told me the strip club. I asked if it was the same stripper that was all over him the last time he and I were at Magic City. At first, he said "no." Then he cleared his throat, said he wanted to be honest with me, then changed his answer to "yes." I could only shake my head. My stomach started to hurt, but I wanted to hear the truth, so I continued. I asked for her name. His initial response was, "Why does that matter?" But after I insisted and eventually screamed at him, demanding the homewrecker's name, he finally told me, "Blaze."

I couldn't look at him, but I had so many more questions. And no one was leaving until they *all were* answered. The most pressing question I had for Grey was, "Why did you ask her to have your baby if she was just something to fuck?" Out of everything I had overheard on the phone, that night he stood me up, which was without question, the most hurtful. I could immediately see in his eyes that he didn't want to answer the question. But it wasn't because he didn't want to tell the truth. Instead, it was because he knew that the truth was really going to hurt me; and it did.

Grey went on to confess that after seeing so many of his partners and colleagues bring their kids around, showing them the ropes of this business, it got him to thinking that he wanted to be able to pass down his legacy and his dream to his own children; his own blood children. He said adopting a child was not the same as having a child with your blood flowing through them and your genetic makeup. He also said he wanted to experience that, if he had the opportunity to do so. That night, my husband said a lot more. I just sat there, listened and quietly wrestled with myself to hold back the tears.

Greyson continued to talk for about twenty minutes. He told me how much he loved me and how much I meant to him, even though he didn't always show it. He said that he did not want to lose me as his wife, insisting that Blaze meant absolutely nothing to him. He expressed that she was just a really cool chic and the only reason he could see himself having a child with her was that she was open to the "arrangement." The arrangement being: she would have a child for Greyson, since his wife, me, couldn't have one for him. Before he could even finish his sentence, I screamed, "Are you fucking kidding me!" I could not believe that he dared to share with another woman, something that was so personal and private to me. Then, to act like they were doing me a favor by fucking each other, I was beyond pissed and highly insulted.

At that point, I had heard enough. I was done with them all. I told Grey to get his ass out of my truck.

Still, he kept pressing. He insisted there would be no romantic or further sexual involvement between him and Blaze. He also felt the need to add, that no matter how good a woman looked, he could never be seriously involved with one who sold her body for a living. I chuckled on the inside at the irony of that statement. But I also thought to myself, *Oh, but you'd intentionally get one pregnant, even though you're a married man, with such high standards? Whatever you idiot."*

Before I could force Grey out, he ended his rant by saying he didn't want another woman. He just wanted us to have a baby of our own. Just as I was about to go off again and tell him that what he was saying made absolutely no sense, he interrupted me. He said we could make an appointment to see a fertility specialist to explore our options and maybe even consider a surrogate. A real surrogate, not a Magic City special surrogate. We had never really discussed any of these options before because Grey wasn't interested in having any kids. At least that's what I thought.

Ultimately, Grey admitted that his actions and approach to the situation were really fucked up. After he apologized some more, he followed up by saying that on the night he had me waiting at home, he had been really horny all day, and just so "happened" to run into Blaze. He said the timing of the situation just got the best of him. The bowl of *BS* was really overflowing, but I didn't let it get me worked up again. Lastly, he ended by telling me that Blaze was on birth control and that he really was just "talking shit," when I heard him say what he said that night. He knew she couldn't really get pregnant.

By the end of our conversation, I felt a little better. So I decided to come home that night. All my clothes and things were already in the trunk. I was still a little hurt by it all. Actually, it still hurt a lot. However, Grey seemed really sincere about wanting to make things work between us. I can't deny it; inside I was super excited about going to see a fertility specialist. But I didn't let Grey know that. Instead, I acted like it wasn't a big deal. Yet, the truth was, the very thought of even possibly being able to be a mommy gave me butterflies.

◊

The next day, I made an appointment for us to see a fertility specialist. They penciled us in for the following week. When the day came, Grey was acting all nervous. I had to tell him to relax like ten times. He was concerned that his sperm count might be too low or that he couldn't conceive a child, now that he really wanted to. At least that's the reason he gave me.

The doctor discussed all of our possible options but advised we'd each have to submit some specimen samples and be examined before determining next steps. After a few weeks and more testing on my side, it was determined that Grey's sperm was up and ready for the challenge, so were my eggs! But as we already knew, I wouldn't be able to carry the baby. We'd have to go with a surrogate, and that process would be both extensive and expensive.

After a few weeks, Grey didn't seem as excited about our baby venture. I figured maybe it was about the money, so I didn't press the issue too much. I knew we could afford it, but it would put a small dent into our savings. Therefore, we didn't need to rush it. We needed to plan some things out regarding our soon-to-be life-changing decision. I was still over-the-moon elated that having a baby was even a possibility. Well, so I thought.

◊

A couple of months later, I was in class, having show-and-tell with my students. We were having a really fun time. Then I got a call from the front office. The kids were really loud as they laughed amongst each other, so I couldn't make out exactly what was said. I only heard, "in the front office." I assumed I must have had a delivery, probably more flowers from Grey. So I popped into Mrs. Cagle's classroom to ask if she could keep an eye on my classroom. Then I made my way to the front office.

As I walked up there, I prepared myself to deal with the ladies in the front office. They were crazy about

Grey. They thought he was so awesome because he was always sending me flowers. Little did they know it was because he was always messing up. It was a big deal to them though. Most of the time they'd do or say something dramatic when I walked in like "TA-DAAAA!" It made me blush, but I really didn't care for all the attention.

Approaching the office, I realized I didn't see a floral bouquet sitting on top of the counter. Usually, it would be visible through the office window from the outside hall. In that instance, I just figured Grey hadn't sent me flowers after all; though it would have been a nice gesture. Then, I wondered why they called me up to the front office near the end of the school day, leaving a classroom full of busy, bouncing first graders? Could it not wait?

When I walked into the front office, Mrs. Deller greeted me. She's always the sweetest. Before I could even ask, she pointed behind me and said "You have a visitor." Completely caught off guard, I spun around and could not believe who was seated in the chair; right there, across from me. It was Blaze.

Though fully clothed, I recognized her face and super full lips immediately, even though I had only seen her once before, under really dim lights. My heart dropped. *What the fuck is this bitch doing up here at my job? How does she even know where I work? I'm going to fucking kill Greyson!* Those were all the immediate thoughts that raced through my mind as I stood there in total shock. She stood up and extended her hand to shake mine. She was towering over me, just as she had when I first saw her in the strip club, but this time her heels were only about five inches tall. She politely introduced herself and told me her name was Tiffany. Then she said she just wanted to leave some real estate papers with me. "Your hubby, Greyson, asked me to drop these off here with you since I'd be in the area today." I could see the evil in her eyes as she handed me the folder.

Still a little confused, I just went with the flow. I was hoping that my uninvited guest wasn't about to do anything that would embarrass me or tarnish my image in any way. I definitely didn't want to have to fight her ass, but I would have if I had to. That would have definitely gone down in the school books' history at Narvie J. Harris Elementary: "Two-time Teacher of the Year, Noel Greyson, gets arrested following front office brawl." There was no way I was going to let that happen, so I quickly decided that no matter what, I wasn't going to let Blaze bring me out of character.

All kinds of questions were running through my mind, but I knew the nosey office staff was probably listening. So I asked "Tiffany" if we could step outside. She smiled and said, "No, actually I have to run, I just wanted to leave those papers with you." She shook my hand again, said it was nice to meet me, and left.

I didn't have to take my silver hoops off after all. I was relieved, but still extremely pissed. I already knew that there was something hideous attached to her visit, and it was inside that folder.

As I made my way back to the classroom, I was anxious to see what was inside the folder, but since we only had about forty-five minutes left to the school day, I figured I'd just wait. I had a strong feeling that what was inside that folder was going to ruin my day. In less than an hour, that feeling was confirmed.

When the final bell rang, and all of my students were gone, I retrieved the folder from my desk drawer. A queasy feeling came over me as I opened it and saw a handwritten note. It read:

Hi Mrs. Greyson,

I'm glad we finally got a chance to meet. I hate to be the bearer of bad news, but there's something you need to know. First off, my name is Tiffany, but some know me as Blaze. Your husband and I have been seeing each other for a while now, and I was under the impression that you all were getting a divorce, but apparently, that isn't the case anymore. Kevin is a manipulative jerk, and you're a fool if you stay with him after all of this. In case you didn't know it, I am pregnant with his baby. This is something we planned, and I also thought we were planning to be together but looks like that has changed.

Anyway, he rented a condo for my three-year-old daughter and me a few months back, and I guess now it will be for "our" new baby too. Good thing we got a three-bedroom. ;)

I'm sure you probably think I'm lying, so behind this letter, you'll find a copy of the lease agreement, in both of our names and also confirmation of my pregnancy from my doctor's office.

Take care,

Tiffany

Sure enough, the lease was there, signed six months prior in the names of Tiffany Bilox and Kevin Greyson. The pregnancy documents were there too. I could feel my face tighten up as my lips began to tremble. I just stared blankly at what was before my eyes. I didn't cry though. I couldn't. I don't think I had any more tears left in me.

◊

The ride home was a long one. I didn't even bother to call Greyson. I was in no mood to do the drama nor hear his lies. I stopped and picked a bottle of wine and some hot wings. When I got home, I showered, then ate and watched a movie; Purple Rain. I still didn't call Greyson, and he hadn't called me, but I was sure to leave the folder and all of its contents spread out on the kitchen counter. I wanted to make sure he saw it, whenever he decided to come home.

I fell asleep on the sofa and was awaken by the sound of keys rambling at the door. I knew it was Greyson, so I jumped up and made my way to the bedroom before he could see me. I pretended like I was sleeping. I could hear him make his way into the kitchen. Then there was total silence for a few minutes. Suddenly, out of nowhere, I heard a glass shatter against the wall as he shouted, "That fucking bitch! I hate that black raggedy ass bitch!" He repeated it like five times, as he stormed around. It scared me. However, not enough to keep me in bed. So I made my way to the kitchen where Greyson was.

When I got in there, he was sitting on the floor, pressed up against the wall, amongst broken pieces of glass. I just stood there and stared at him. He couldn't look at me though. A couple of minutes went by before he even said anything. He just kept clearing his throat as he stared down at the floor. I wasn't about to let him even try to play the victim this time.

Before I knew it, I had blurted out, "I fucking hate you!" As deserving as he was to be hated, he was totally caught off guard to hear that come from me. It was enough to make him speak though. But all he had to say was, "I know you do. You should." Then he dropped his head. That wasn't good enough for me. I was not about to let him just sit there and play the victim in any capacity. Then I became angry, boiling over-the-top angry.

I started picking up glasses and forcefully throwing them against the wall, as I shouted every profane word that came to mind. Think I even made up a few. I was mad! Shattered pieces of glass were flying everywhere. Before I knew it, I couldn't stop. I had snapped and lost all control. It scared the shit out of

Grey. He jumped up, but his timing was wrong. His head met the path of one of the flying glasses at full speed. It split open. Blood was gushing everywhere. I was terrified!

I ran to get some towels to put over the gaping cut on his forehead, but the bleeding wouldn't stop. Luckily, we don't live too far from a hospital, so I was able to rush him to the emergency room. He had to get twenty-seven stitches in his head. I felt horrible.

◊

Grey was home all day for a few days following that night. We got a chance to talk. He did his usual; apologized, confessed, and made more empty promises. It turns out Blaze was already pregnant with his baby on that night I heard them screwing over the phone. I don't know how long he thought he was going to be able to live that lie. Men are so fucking stupid. He got her the place because he felt her old apartment wasn't good enough for his future seed to occupy. He didn't tell me, but I'm sure he made Blaze some promises. Maybe they really were planning to be together. Then perhaps he changed his mind. I don't know. Either way, when she realized he really wasn't trying to make her "number one" in his life, it pissed her off. So she came to see me.

I felt so bad about splitting Greyson's head open that I just threw my hands up at the circumstances. I didn't feel like going through all the questions or hearing more of his lies than I had to. I was hurt. Still am. But sadly, I've gotten so accustomed to feeling this way that I almost just feel numb. There's a good chance that Grey and I will end up going our separate ways, especially after his daughter arrives. But there's so much to factor in. There's so much I'd be giving up. I don't think he's messing around with Blaze anymore because she absolutely hates the fact that he's still over here with me. I think that's probably part of the reason I haven't left him yet, even after all of this. I don't want her to think that she won. I'm still the "Mrs." you bitch.

Blaze will just have to deal with all the consequences that result from knowingly and intentionally getting pregnant by a married man, with her dirty, low-class ass. And I'll just have to deal with consequences of loving Greyson too much and perhaps not loving myself enough. Greyson isn't off the hook though. He will pay the price for all his dirt too, as God sees fit.

"We" have a baby on the way, if I stay. So as much as I feel like I hate Blaze and Greyson too, depending on the day, I have to accept it. It is what it is. Plus, I have a deep-rooted love for babies and children.

They're so innocent and pure when they're young. None of them asked to be here, despite how they got here. It's our job to protect them. That's why I became a teacher. And that's why I can't find it in my heart to wish evil upon or hate Grey's unborn child, even if I hate him. I'll just have to find a way to deal with all of this as best as I can. Yes, what my husband has done is beyond dirty, but all babies are a gift from God, and that makes them *clean*.

7

Sometimes you get what you want. Sometimes you get what you need. And sometimes, you get what you get. I believe most of the time, it's the latter.

I'm starting to get used to him not being around. It's not like we were seeing each other a whole lot these days anyway. To be honest, I got used to the loneliness quite some time ago. With Greyson always working (or doing whatever), our quality time has become less and less over the years. Much of that has to do with his career taking off. As he's produced more records, for bigger artists especially, Grey has made his way into bigger, more prominent circles within the music industry. In turn, our circle of love, and our rings I suppose have become less important to him. Well, maybe not even important at all.

I didn't want him to go, but it was too much of a dagger in my heart for him to stay. I tried my best to push through and forgive my husband for being such a playboy, for being a liar, and for being a cheater. I know he didn't deserve my forgiveness, but I gave it to him anyway; time and time again. Then he turned right around and slapped me in the face with it; hard enough to knock me off my feet. He broke my heart into a million pieces. And still, I tried to do the impossible, and forgive my husband for impregnating another woman, or rather a trifling-stank-bitch, in Tiffany's case. Either way, she's now officially his one and only, "baby momma." It makes me cringe to even think that out loud. But, it is what it is. She beat me. And I hate her for it. Nonetheless, that home-wrecking whore won. I'm Greyson's wife, and I wasn't able, nor really even given the opportunity, to try to be the one thing for him that would have meant everything in the world to me; the mother of his child.

There is no possible way that I could ever truly express the degree of hurt I'm experiencing behind all of this. It feels like someone is just mushing crushed up pieces of glass into my heart, over and over again. Then standing there to see just how much I'll bleed.

◊

I did everything within my power to tough it out with Grey. However, when it came down to the last straw, it was only because he had somehow convinced me that he *still* wanted me to everything and everyone. If only for two seconds, I believed him. He made believe that he was still in love with me and that he wanted our marriage to survive, despite the sticky situation. Crushingly, all of that changed the day Nyla arrived.

We were at home one Sunday night, watching *Purple Rain*. I was happy that we were having a little cuddle-up time together. We'd ordered in for dinner; medium hot wings, sprinkled with lemon pepper, with home-made, adult beverages on the side. Just as I was about to doze off in Grey's lap, I started hearing his phone vibrate like crazy. He tried to act like he didn't hear it at first, but it was annoying the hell out of me, so I made him get it.

He grudgingly walked over to the breakfast bar and fished his phone out of his sweatpants that were laying across a chair. When he looked down at the screen, I heard him murmur "Fuck!" Then he headed to our bedroom. As usual, my heart dropped. "What was it this time?" I wondered as I rolled my eyes. Then, within what felt like a few seconds, Grey rushed back out of the room, fully dressed. He said he had to go down to the hospital right away because Tiffany was in labor. This terrified him because Tiffany was only thirty-two weeks along. He knew she was in labor too soon and didn't want anything to go wrong with his baby girl. I swear, when Grey raced out of the door that night, he took with him the last bit of hope remaining for our marriage; annihilating it into the asphalt pavement of the parking garage, as he fish-tailed his way out.

I must have felt sick to my stomach for the remainder of that night. I knew by morning, my life would forever change, drastically; more than it already had. I hated the very thought of it. This unwelcome and unwarranted reality was coming to fruition, and all I could do was just deal with it; whatever "dealing with it" meant. That scared me the most.

It wasn't until around 8 o'clock the following morning that I finally heard from Grey. His voice sounded pretty shaken up. At first, I couldn't tell if something was wrong with the baby or if it was just hard for him to speak because he was delivering news of his newborn child, to his wife. After a minute or two, I had to coach it out of him. I asked him what was wrong. He told me the baby was ok for the most part but had a few minor issues. She would have to stay in the NICU for a month or so, until she could breathe on her own, and take all her feedings by mouth since she came so early. He added that she only weighed about three and a half pounds. At that point, I wasn't sure what to say. So, I said nothing. I just held the phone to my ear, and let a few tears escape.

My stomach was twisted is ten knots, but then I brought myself to say it, "Congrats on your new baby girl Greyson. I'm sure she'll be fine." Oh, my God! It hurt so bad to say that. He knew it too, but he also knew that he couldn't change what was already done. Therefore, he didn't bother apologizing to me again. Lord knows I'd received a gazillion apologies, in all the weeks and months leading up to that day. So instead, Grey said something else. I'm sure he thought it was going to make me feel better about the whole ordeal, but it didn't. In fact, it made me feel worse.

"You want to know her name?" Grey asked in a raspy, please-clear-your-throat kind of voice. "Sure," I replied. But really, I was thinking, "Oh God, here comes more foolishness." Then he told me he named his daughter "Nyla Belle." It snatched my breath away, like a Chicago wind in the middle of January. I couldn't believe it. Why the hell would he do that? How could he do that? And more importantly, did Tiffany have anything to do with it? I could come up with at least three reasons why she would have agreed to it; the biggest one being to hurt me. I was absolutely disgusted. In the awkward silence, Grey had to know why.

Years prior, I had shared with Grey that my mom used to always tell me about how she was extremely torn between naming me Noel or Nyla when I was born. She absolutely loved both names so much so, that she was ready to name me "Nyla Noel." But, my dad wanted me to have his mom's name, as my middle name. She had passed away earlier that year. Therefore, my mom didn't put up a fight. She was happy to do so. However, to decide on my first name, they ended up flipping a coin. With that, I was named "Noel Belle."

As a kid, I always promised mom that if I ever had a child of my own one day, I would name her "Nyla Belle." She adored the idea, especially since she was so fond of my Grandma Belle, long before she transcended into heaven. She was like a mother to my mom. Unfortunately, my grandma on my mom's side, passed away when my mother was only four-years-old. After that, it was just her, my aunt and uncles, and my grandpa. He never remarried. Then sadly, he died when my mom was fourteen. At that time, Grandma Belle was just a sweet neighbor who helped my mom and her siblings with whatever they needed. She cooked for them and everything. Years later, her son asked my mom for her hand in marriage. But Belle loved my mom long before she became her daughter-in-law and vice versa. My mom loved the name "Nyla Belle" just as much as she did "Noel Belle." That's why the name meant so much to me. Then Grey went and did that shit. I could not believe it.

◊

In the weeks that followed Nyla's birth, Grey was at the hospital around the clock; right by her side. And right by Tiffany's side as well. I understood that he had to be there for his child, but it angered me at the same time. It was like he had completely forgotten all about me, about everything that he had promised me. And he didn't care. Days would go by, and I wouldn't see him. He claimed to be spending nights at the hospital. Whether or not that was entirely true, I don't know. But it's what he said.

When I'd leave for work in the morning, most of the time, Grey wasn't there. I guess sometime during the day he'd pop in and shower. Then he'd take off for work. From work, he would often go straight back to the hospital, where he stayed for the night. Wash, rinse, repeat. Again, that's what he led me to believe.

That routine went on for almost two months. During that time, communication between Grey and me was almost nonexistent. I can't even say that it was because he could feel my resentment, which I had plenty of, but we weren't around each other enough for him to really feel my constantly resurfacing bitterness towards him. Rarely were we breathing the same air. It's like in the blink of an eye, his life was all about Nyla, and perhaps Tiffany too; but certainly, not about me.

At first, he would voluntarily text me updates on Nyla's progress and send me pictures of her. The pics only made my gut wrench. She's the splitting image of Greyson. He couldn't deny her even if he wanted to. Although a real cutie-pie, Nyla was hard to look at. So very quickly, looking at her pics got to be too much. I guessed when Grey realized that I would never have more than a one-word reply, outside of "cute" or "nice," when he sent me snapshots of Nyla, he decided to stop sharing things like that with me altogether. Really, he stopped talking about Nyla period, at least to me.

I started drinking very heavily during that time. And it has since continued. My tolerance for alcohol has shot through the roof. I can go through a bottle of vodka every other day, or a bottle and a half of wine in one. And not the small bottles either; the size you'd bring to someone's housewarming party. Somehow, though, with only a few isolated exceptions, I'm always able to get up and make my way to school, on time. My first-graders are definitely a welcomed distraction from all the chaotic mess that *always* seems to be going on in my life. And as far as my students, colleagues, and neighbors know, Mr. Greyson and I are still very much in love, and happily married. I even sent myself flowers "from him" last month for my birthday. Because I didn't think he would remember to, but surprisingly he did. My getting two separate deliveries, from my husband, really impressed the ladies in the front office at my school. They still think Grey is one of the best husbands in the world. Hopefully, they'll never know the truth.

◊

On the day Nyla was discharged from the hospital, Grey asked if I wanted to meet her. I told him "no." But I honestly wasn't trying to be rude. I had purposefully stayed away from the hospital. I knew how I felt about Tiffany and didn't want to risk running into her. I had never physically seen Nyla in person, but I also wasn't in a rush to to see her.

Even though I've tried my best to suppress these toxic feelings of mine, I simply cannot. They're even more prevalent now. I'll probably always hate Tiffany's ass. She's taken so much away from me. And now, I think it's safe to say that I hate Greyson too.

When I told him that I didn't want to meet Nyla, I wasn't trying to be mean. I just wasn't ready to commit to seeing his "love child" in person, especially in one impromptu conversation over the phone. I needed to get my head right. I just needed a little time. For heaven's sake, he sprung this on me while I was on my lunch break at work? I had no idea that Nyla had even been cleared to go home. Last I heard she was having trouble with her breathing or something like that. You'd think Greyson, of all people, would understand the sensitivity of the circumstances from my shoes. You'd think he would have had more compassion for me and my feelings. Nope, he didn't. It was all about him and his baby girl.

In a matter of minutes, I was rendered speechless. Grey completely went off on me! He cursed me out like I was some mad dog in the streets trying to attack him. He told me that if his daughter wasn't welcome in our home, then neither was he. Then he told me he was leaving. By the time I got home from work, a good third of his clothes and shoes had been removed from our closet. I didn't have to guess whose closet they'd been moved to. The level of devastation and defeat I felt at that moment was indescribable.

That day, my world completely shifted. I had been beaten to a bloody, mangled pulp. I was battered, bruised, and beyond tired. It was from that decrepit valley that I decided I wasn't going to fight for my marriage anymore. I decided that I wasn't going to let my ugly life and circumstances kick my ass anymore. I decided that I would no longer try to make Greyson love me the way I felt he should have. Instead, I was going to get completely lost in loving myself. And as far as my husband leaving me to go and build a life with some other woman, and their out-of-wedlock child, I decided to just let him go. I decided to let it ALL go. As much as it hurt then, and still hurts now, I know I can't let it kill me. So, with all the extra alone time to think, I've been writing and filling up my song journal to help free my mind and ease the heartache, if only a little bit. Who knows, I might even record my songs one day. Doubt it, but who knows. After all, I think I just penned my best song yet. In fact, I've adopted it as my new personal mantra. I'm especially dedicating this one to Grey, our shitty marriage, and to any and every bad thing that has ever happened to me in life. I'm so over all of it. I've decided to entitle this song, *I Don't Give a Fuck Anymore...*

8

What a crazy, yet incredible weekend it has been. I can't remember the last time I drank, smiled, and laughed so hard, within a 48-hour period. It's been that great. And very much needed, may I add. Heaven knew I had to put the tears on pause for a minute and just laugh. I was sick of them staining my pillowcase every night. It's a wonder that I didn't die from dehydration. I had cried that much.

I don't know what to say about my life right now, other than it's crazy as fuck, in every possible way. I don't even know who I am anymore, besides a woman who's just trying to deal with it all. Grey and I are separated, but not legally. I can't even begin to guess what the future holds for us, but I assume the rotten bastard's doing just dandy. It's been a couple of weeks since I've seen or spoken to Grey. However, he did eventually apologize for blowing up on me and leaving the way he did. He admitted that he fucked up; acknowledging that, unfortunately, this time it wasn't something he could just "fix" by sending me flowers or by buying me an expensive piece of jewelry. Nope, this "fuck-up" was way too big for that remedy.

Greyson said he felt bad about everything. But in true Grey fashion, he then followed that up with, "But you know, it is what it is." That only aggravated me. He can be such a calloused dick at times. He claims that he doesn't want to divorce me, but at the same time, he understands if I decide to divorce him. However, he has reassured me that, in the meantime, I can continue living in the condo if I choose to since it's in both of our names. He also said he would keep paying the mortgage, for as long as I need him to. Gee thanks.

When Grey removed the last of his things from our home, I felt like I had fallen into an episode of the Twilight Zone. For days, maybe even weeks, it felt like I was just spinning; like I was only partially functioning and existing. The sudden and rash magnitude of Grey's exit was impossible for me to understand. I mean, just like that, he left me. And he wasn't the least bit apologetic or remorseful when he did it, at least not genuinely. I felt so betrayed. I felt like this was his plan all along. His dirty, rotten-to-the-core, trifling ass laid with me and lied to me, like a wolf in sheep's clothing; day after day, month after month, year after year. And sadly, I can't even begin to understand why. Looking back, though, when my father decided that he would be happier elsewhere, he did my sweet mommy the same way. He just up and left; just like that. Grey is no different; I don't think many men are. On that note, I can't speak for tomorrow, but I can say, that on this day I hate men; all of them.

Now that I got that out, enough about my present hatred towards the male species. Let's get back to my weekend. The weather was beautiful; not too hot, not too cold, just nice and breezy, with a certain crispness in the air. It was pretty much what you'd expect Fall to feel like in the south. Fall has always been my most favorite season. It's usually the time of year when I'm happiest. Fortunately, this weekend got that trend going again.

It was Friday night, and I decided that I didn't want to stay in the house sulking for another entire weekend. I had to get out and go somewhere but didn't want to go alone. Since I didn't have many friends and didn't want to hang out with anyone who even remotely knew Grey, my options were limited. For a moment, I wished my old best friend, Nicole, lived closer. I haven't seen her in ages, and I still haven't told her about *all* that has happened between Grey and me, not even about the baby. I'm not ready to tell her about that yet. So maybe it's good that she's hundreds of miles away. Still, I needed a date.

Since I was not looking for a romantic kind of date, I certainly had no desire to go out with a man. What I needed was a woman. I needed a fun drinking companion; someone I could hang out with, and just laugh. I needed someone who wasn't too unrefined, but exciting, and who would also be available on a Friday night, on short notice. I just wanted to forget about all my cares for a few hours. It was that simple. But while I knew what I wanted, I wasn't so sure on how to go about making it happen.

The only thing I could think to do at first was to start searching the internet using key terms like "girls night out" and "women for women." Of course, that directed me to a bunch of dating websites for lesbian and bisexual women. Since that wasn't quite what I was looking for, I quickly became frustrated. Plus, all of them were asking me to build a profile with my picture attached to it. That was not about to happen. So, I continued to poke around until about 9'oclock. Then, I remembered that on one occasion, before Grey and I were married, we put an ad up on Craigslist to find another single woman to join us for a threesome. Although I said "we," Grey was the one who orchestrated all of it. But ultimately, we received several responses, and fast.

Since Craigslist has different categories in the personals section, I figured I'd just post a quick and simple ad under "w4w" section, and spell out exactly what I was looking for, so there wouldn't be any confusion:

W4W – Drinks on me TONIGHT!!! – Atlanta

Recently separated from my husband. Would love to get out the house TONIGHT to shake off the blues. I just need a fun and friendly companion for cocktails, conversation, and laughs. Drinks on meeee if you'll be my date!!!

Please be 25 y/o or older and CLASSY. Reply ASAP if interested. Your pic gets mine. No pic. No reply.

Women ONLY. No men. No couples.

I kept it short and sweet, and within five minutes, I had gotten over ten replies to my ad. Two of the replies were pics of some guys' dicks, so I didn't even bother reading what they had to say. But other than that, the other responses seemed quite legitimate. And they kept coming in. It gave me butterflies. I was excited!

I hardly expected to get all the responses I ended up receiving. I think leading with "free drinks" played a huge part in that. However, since it was getting later and later by the minute, I knew I wouldn't have time to read through all the messages, and then go back and forth with pic exchanges for each of them. Therefore, I ended up agreeing to meet the third person who responded. Her name was Paige. She was an attractive woman, close to my age, and looked fashionably diva-luscious in all her pictures. But best of all, she was also an elementary school teacher. That sealed the deal for me!

After voice verifying and chatting on the phone for a few, Paige and I agreed to meet at Dugan's, a local sports bar, that was about equal distance between the two of us. I made it there first, so I waited in the parking lot for Paige to arrive. After about ten minutes, a shiny, red Lexus backed into an open parking space next to my SUV. Then my phone rang. It was Paige. She asked if I had made it to the bar yet. I told her I had. Then I looked down into the car parked beside me. A lady was talking on the phone, but looking straight ahead. I asked Paige to look up to her right. Sure enough, it was her. She looked up at me, and we both laughed; both still holding our phones up to our ears. That's when I knew the night was going to be interesting and fun. The fact that both Paige and I were both driving nice cars earning teachers' salaries let me know that she certainly had a story. And the fact that we had just met, only a couple of hours ago, via Craigslist, could only guarantee a stimulating night, filled with cocktails and conversation.

Paige and I exited our vehicles, then hugged each other like two long lost friends; snickering like high school girls. Nothing about the moment felt forced or fake. It was just something about her; I immediately felt like she was my friend. After that, we headed inside and spent the next three hours or so indulging in music, martinis, and awesome conversation. We clicked instantly. I felt like I had known her for years. We talked about some of everything, but mostly about school at first. She teaches the fourth grade.

Then after our first round, we loosened up a bit more. That's when we started talking about our husbands and our very broken marriages.

It was great to just have someone to talk to. More importantly, Paige was someone who could relate to and identify with what I was going through because her story was like mine in a lot of ways. Neither one of us feared being judged by the other. We were open books, if only for that night. And it felt great.

As the night carried on, the cocktails and conversation continued. We people-watched, we laughed, and we even hit the dance floor a few times. Then we talked about each other's hair, as we started to sweat out our curls. Paige's hair was even longer than mine. It reached her lower back. She accredited it to both her Asian mom and her thick-maned African American father. Her hair was long, jet black, and beautiful, just like her. She was really beautiful; inside and out.

Before we knew it, it was three o'clock in the morning. The bar was closing, and we were both ridiculously drunk. Fortunately, neither one of us felt sick, though. Because of that, we decided that we'd go to the Waffle House, just a few blocks up, to put something on our stomachs before that changed. However, we both knew we needed to sit still for a minute, and sober up a little, before driving anywhere. That's when we headed back out to the parking lot and jumped into my Range Rover.

I cracked open the sunroof a little bit, and we both reclined our seats back and listened to Jagged Edge's station on Pandora. The first song that came on was "Gotta Be." It made me cry because it made me think about Grey. But it made Paige laugh at me. She reached over and double squeezed my right boob while making a honking sound. The brute awkwardness of it made me laugh. Then she told me everything was going to be ok because we had found each other. And for some reason, something deep inside of me believed she was right, despite our inebriated states.

Out of nowhere, came a forceful, banging on my window! It scared the crap out of Paige and me. I almost peed on myself. We were both caught off guard; still reclined in our seats and very much discombobulated. We'd fallen asleep. With barely one eye open, we peered out the front window and saw that it was daylight outside. There was a police cruiser parked in front of us and a police officer at my door. Immediately, I pulled myself together, I took that as my que to roll down the window.

Officer Simms greeted us. While Paige and I were asleep in my truck, the officer just so happened to be patrolling the area. He thought it was strange to see two vehicles parked in the sports bar's parking lot at that hour, so he decided to check things out. Lucky for us he did, and even luckier, we weren't harmed in any way while both were completely knocked out and unguarded.

After the officer pulled off, Paige and I couldn't help but laugh at ourselves. Then I told her she needed to check her phone because her husband was probably wondering where the hell she was. She told me that she was certain he wasn't. I just left it at that. I was still too drunk to care.

By that time, we were both starving. So, we put our respective cars in motion and headed to the "House." I couldn't get my order in with the waitress fast enough. As soon as we were seated, I ordered a batch of loaded hash browns; scattered, smothered, covered, chunked, and capped. They were hot and delicious. By far the best I've had. Paige ordered the same, but took hers up a notch, and had hers "topped" with chili.

Being in a much quieter environment and semi-sober gave Paige and I the opportunity to converse and learn a little more about each other. I couldn't help but wonder what was up with her husband. Like, how could he not be blowing up her phone after she didn't come home last night? I had already shared that Grey and I were separated and weren't living together, so that was my estranged husband's excuse for not giving a damn. However, from what Paige shared, I only knew that her husband was an IT Director at some big dotcom company and that they'd been married for at least few years. I knew that like mine, her marriage had been super shitty for the past year, but I did not know the details of her "shitty-ness." Since Paige had been pretty transparent up to that point, I decided to ask her about it. Her initial reaction almost made me wish I hadn't. She put down her fork, shook her head, and paused before answering my question. Then she asked me to promise not to judge her. Without any hesitation, I promised.

Paige revealed to me that she and her husband had an "open" marriage. She said it was something she agreed to a few months ago, in hopes of saving her marriage. The way it works for them is basically her husband leaves the house every Friday night, to be with whomever and do whatever, and doesn't return home until Sunday. Per their agreement, Paige cannot question his whereabouts or any other details for that matter but is free to do what she wants, with whoever she wants, while her husband is away. There was only one exception; no men.

I was floored. I felt so bad for her, even though that type of arrangement had my husband's name written all over it. I reached out to grab Paige's hand. I wanted to console her and let her know that I would never judge her or think bad of for doing what she felt she needed to do to hold on to her husband and marriage. I understood. What I didn't understand, was her abruptly pulling her hand away, before I could grab it. She reached for her phone instead.

She told me there was more, but I couldn't even begin to think of what "more" could be. Then she handed me her phone. On the screen, was a picture of Paige wrapped up in the arms of a white man. They both were smiling from ear to ear. It was a great picture. I couldn't help but wonder what the big deal was. That's when Paige told me that the person pictured with her was her husband. My response was, "Aww! You two make a cute couple!" They honestly did. "Did you think I was going to care that he was white or something?" Her response was, "No, I didn't. But that's not why I showed you the picture."

I was totally confused at that point. And Paige just sat there staring at me, as if sitting on eggshells. That only made it more awkward and confusing. With that, I continued to analyze the picture on her phone, although I wasn't sure what I was looking for. That's when Paige whispered, "Look closer." Then I saw it! My mouth dropped before I could catch myself. Paige just buried her face in her hands. She was embarrassed, but truthfully, she had no reason to be.

"I didn't know how to tell you," Paige whispered. She went on to say that she just wanted to get out of the house the night before. She just wanted to get her mind off the conditions of her home, life, and marriage. She wasn't expecting to meet a new best friend or anything. I felt the same way. I wholeheartedly believe that we were meant to meet each other that night; because we desperately needed each other that night.

Paige told me that no one at her school knew and that she had pretty much distanced herself from her family because she couldn't even bear the thought of them knowing her reality. She felt like it was her business, and if she chose to share it or not to share it, it was entirely her prerogative. I agreed. Like me, she was just a more private person. Plus, no one wants to feel like they're being judged by other people because their life or lifestyle isn't considered the "norm." I reassured Paige that I was ok with her being who she was and that we were going to be besties regardless. She laughed and then came over to my side of the booth and gave me a big hug. I warned her not to grab my ass, but she did it anyway. We continued to talk and laugh it up over coffee. I could tell Paige had found peace in my presence, knowing that I understood why she still wasn't quite ready to let the whole world know that she was a lesbian.

We spent the remainder of the weekend together. Paige went home, grabbed some clothes, and then crashed at my condo until late Sunday afternoon. We had a blast. We shopped, cooked, drank, watched movies, talked about everything under the sun, and we even smoked a couple of joints (courtesy of Paige of course). She got me so freaking high, then we hit up the world-famous Clermont Lounge, Atlanta's oldest strip club. That was one ridiculously fun and crazy experience all on its own. I'd certainly do it again, but I don't think I could ever eat there.

Yes, this weekend has been awesome. I hated to see Paige go. But we both have papers to grade and lessons to plan by Monday morning, so our fun had to end. It's okay because we planned to do it all over again next weekend. And I can't wait! When I think about all the time I've spent crying, stressing, or even caring about people and things that have caused me more harm than anything, it feels good to just have an ounce of peace in my heart and the tingle of happiness again. It felt good to laugh without restraint. It felt good to be spontaneous and just go with the flow. It felt good to just live and let all the bullshit go. Ultimately, it feels good not to give a fuck anymore. It feels damn good.

9

I'm not a lesbian. Not saying that there's anything wrong with being a lesbian. Just saying I'm not one. Yes, I may dibble and dabble here and there, but that's because my life is superiorly fucked up right now, and I welcome any comforting distraction. Either way, it doesn't define who I am because I'm not a lesbian. I'm just me; a confined free spirit, in search of love and happiness. And, at this point, I'm willing to accept it, however it comes. It could be with a man or with a woman. Honestly, I don't care anymore. I just want to be happy; again.

Two years ago, my husband left me for another woman. Well, first he cheated on me, with an exotic dancer. Then he got her pregnant. Then, he left. It's been the longest two years of my life. I wouldn't wish it on my worst enemy. Okay, I'm lying. I would wish it upon my worst enemy; Tiffany. That bitch deserves to feel all the never-ending hurt and pain that I've been forced to endure, and then some.

Tiffany is the trout-mouth tramp that my husband, Greyson, left me for two years ago. But let him tell it, he didn't leave me to be with her. Instead, he left me because he wanted to be in his new-born daughter's life. And considering the circumstances, he didn't think that would've been pleasantly possible, had he stayed with me. Whatever, I just roll my eyes at the whole situation, every time I think about it.

◊

Things have been crazy, to say the least. I ended up transferring to a new elementary school, not long after Greyson and I officially separated. I needed a fresh start, at least in some capacity. Plus, I felt like there was a little too much whispering going on inside the teacher's lounge, regarding my personal affairs. Of course, it was probably just my own paranoia. Still, the shit fest that was going on in my life was getting to be too much to hide, so I had to go.

What's even crazier, is that even after two years, Grey and I still aren't divorced. He never filed, neither did I. He also kept his promise to keep paying the mortgage on our Buckhead condo, where I reside. I figure if his baby momma's dumb, trifling ass doesn't care that he's still married to me, then why the hell should I? After all, it's not like I have much of a love life going on right now anyway. And technically, he is still my husband. However, with all the bad blood between us, Greyson and I don't speak very often. But, I'll admit it, we have hooked up on a few occasions, to have some hot, steamy, meaningless sex. I will also admit that each time, I try to suck and fuck the shit out of him; more so out of my spite for Tiffany, than for anything else. Ultimately though, I always end up regretting it; usually right as Grey's standing over me, squirting his cum all over my face and breasts. Maybe a small part of me wants my husband to come back home, but the other ninety-five percent of me is screaming, "Fuck you! You heartless, douche-bag ass NIGGA! I fucking hate you! I don't care how big your dick is or how good it feels, I'm fucking DONE with your ass!" That's until I find myself fucking him again. Go figure.

Isn't it funny how a man can fuck over one woman after another, and still manage to sleep well at night? It's absolutely bizarre to me. Like clearly, you don't have a conscious. I'm convinced Grey doesn't have one. I have a feeling he sleeps like a baby every night. Meanwhile, I'm secretly over here popping pills, drinking like a fucking sailor, and smoking weed like a new-age hippie, just to fall asleep. And most nights, I do all three. Thankfully, my new students and colleagues have no idea that I'm a borderline alcoholic and quite possibly an addict. I give them no reason to suspect that my life is anything less than copacetic. I'm never late and rarely do I ever miss a day of work. And somehow, I always manage to put on my happy face, all day, every day; until I make it back home.

I've been exploring all kinds of ways to cope. Occasionally, I'll write a song that ties into how I'm feeling, but I don't do it as much anymore. It only makes me think about Grey; more than I need to. I've tried a few dating sites, in hopes that I'd find someone to help me get over Greyson; nothing more, nothing less. However, those experiences have been less than desirable. For starters, dating websites are not discreet at all. I hate the fact that you have to put up a profile picture of yourself, which shows your face. If not, your profile seems suspect and catfish-ish. Therefore, most would probably just keep scrolling past it. At least, that's what I would do. And of course, that defeats the whole purpose. The problem is, anyone can view your profile once it's out there. The last thing I need is Grey, or someone who knows Grey, or someone from my school, or anyone who knows me for that matter, seeing me desperately pleading to be loved on some dating website. Not to mention, it's like a meat market. The excessive inboxes from guys I would never even consider dating is beyond annoying. Then, you have those guys who clearly just want a piece of ass, while the other ones want to get married, as soon as tomorrow. It's all just too much.

A while ago, I did find someone who made me smile again. She was like my best friend, right off the bat. We spent a lot of time together, helping each other cope with the troubles we each were having in our marriages. We joked and laughed so much whenever we were around each other. It didn't matter where we were or what we were doing. Since we both were teachers, we'd often spend our weekends together, grading papers and creating our lesson plans for the upcoming week; all while having cocktails, cooking, and getting high in between. She was my drinking buddy and the reason I've become quite the cannabis enthusiast these days. I loved her. Then, I fell in love with her. I think she fell in love with me too. Then, things got weird; too weird. Then, just like that, she was gone.

◊

I met Paige on a classified ads website, called Craig's List. That night, I was just desperate to get out of the house. I needed to get my mind off Grey, and his many shenanigans. Apparently, Paige was in search of the same. With that, she and I met for drinks at a local bar. Not only did we hang out all night, but we also ended up spending the rest of that weekend together.

From day one, Paige shared with me that she was a lesbian; a married lesbian. I had no problems with it all. At that time, I already had a few girl-on-girl experiences myself, but they'd mostly been while having threesomes with my husband. But even taking that out of the equation, I didn't care that Paige was into women. It never bothered me the least.

Often, when Paige and I would hang out, we'd playfully be a little touchy-feely, especially around the house. It was nothing for us to slap each other on the ass or lay across each other's lap while watching a movie. And I can't tell you how many times we got shit-faced and passed out in the same bed. It never made me feel uncomfortable; not once. In fact, part of me wondered why Paige had never even tried to go "there" with me, especially considering she could have easily blamed it on the alcohol. I mean, I'm cute. However, at the same time, I understood that we had an incredible friendship and we needed each other. We couldn't afford to mess it up. But, somehow, we did. Blame it on me.

I don't know if I had gone too long without having sex or what, but on this particular day, my lady parts were aroused and throbbing. It wasn't even noon yet, and already, I had masturbated like three times. Each time, Paige was present in the sexy scenes in my head. She was doing all sorts of kinky things to me in my mind. The hot, forbidden thoughts made me climax repeatedly. After that, I was convinced; I had to experience the real thing, in real life. I had to experience Paige.

I felt like a man at first. There I was, strategizing on how I was going to seduce my best friend inconspicuously. Part of me felt bad. Then I quickly shook it off. It wasn't like I was going to force her to do anything. After all, she was the lesbian, not me. I was just horny.

Paige and I had plans to get together later that evening. Kevin Hart, one of our most favorite comedians, was going to be at Philips Arena, and we had tickets! I was definitely looking forward to the night's festivities, for more reasons than one.

When Paige arrived to pick me up, she looked amazing. She always looked nice though, but it was especially apparent to me that night. She had on a cute white halter top, that revealed the perfect amount of cleavage and a nice pair of skinny jeans. Immediately, I noticed that she was not wearing a bra, primarily because her headlights were on high beam and poking through her shirt. I couldn't resist the opportunity to jokingly point it out to her while copping a free feel. We both just laughed. But secretly, I wanted her to walk over to me, and kiss me. I at least hoped the evening would end that way.

Before heading out, we did our usual pre-party thing and enjoyed a couple of cocktails and a joint filled with purple Kush. I had no idea that there were so many different types of weed out there. Well, that was before I met Paige. She's definitely a cannabis connoisseur. But, you'd never know it; not just by looking at her. That was one of the many things I loved about her; she was so discreet, just like me.

When it was time for us to head out, we realized we'd gotten much higher and tipsier than we had planned. So, instead of driving, we decided to catch an Uber to the show. It worked out perfectly. I think we laughed the entire way there while flirting with our cutie-pie driver. All in all, we had a pleasurable start to our evening.

The show ended up running late, so afterward, we just grabbed some Chipotle and headed back to my place. Once there, we got our own after party going. We turned the music up and started dancing and taking shots of tequila. Before we knew it, we were four shots in, and I was ready to just come out and tell Paige that I wanted her to come and sit on my face. But, drunk or not, I couldn't bring myself to do it. Instead, I started talking about Greyson, which was the last thing I wanted to do.

Paige and I would always listen and comfort each other whenever one of us was in our feelings about our spouses. That night was no different. Paige listened to me go on and on about Grey for at least an hour. I was drunk, so I was even more emotional. I'm sure I didn't share anything with her that I hadn't shared many times before until I told her that I had recently been sexually intimate with Grey. She was not happy to hear that at all. She hated Grey for all that he'd done to me. I certainly understood why, and I appreciated her anger on my behalf. Still, I had to be honest with her. I knew that continuing to be sexually involved with Grey, even if only once in a while, was stupid, for many reasons. I would never be able to heal or move on as long as I was fucking him. I knew that. However, as I shared with Paige, I didn't have anyone else in my life to satisfy my sexual needs. Granted, I'm not one who must have it all the time. However, when I'm ready, I'm ready. I certainly wasn't trying to hook up with some random guy for a cheap thrill, and run the risk of catching something. At least, that's what I had been telling myself.

I don't know if it was the tequila or what, but Paige was pissed to learn that I was still hooking up with

Grey on occasion, and she let me have it! I'd never seen her so upset. She was cursing and everything. She even attempted to leave, but I wouldn't let her. We'd both had way too many drinks. Eventually, I got her to calm down, even though she was still visibly upset. Ultimately, I ended up throwing her a blanket to sleep on the sofa. Then, I took her car keys, to ensure she didn't sneak out while I was asleep. After that, I headed to my bedroom, shut the door, and passed out.

Around three in the morning, my bedroom door crept open. It was Paige. I just laid there and pretended like I was still asleep. I felt her climb on the other side of the bed. That's where she normally slept whenever she stayed over. Then, after about ten minutes, she moved to the center of the bed. I waited a few minutes, then I shifted my body to the center as well.

Still, I kept my back to her. Not too long after, I felt Paige's hand on my shoulder. It was cold, but I didn't say anything, nor did I move. She gently started to stroke my back. It was extremely soothing. Then, she leaned in, pressing her bare breasts up against my back, and whispered, "I'm so sorry Noel. Please let me make it up to you. Pretty please?" I could still smell the tequila on her breath, but I could not believe what I was hearing. *Was this really about to happen?*

Considering she was topless and had now started running her fingers through my hair, I could only assume that Paige meant that she wanted to make love to me. Well, I was hoping that was the case. Before I could even ask, she gently turned me over onto my back, climbed on top of me and straddled her legs across my waist. Her long, black hair draped over the sides of her breasts, allowing her very erect nipples to highlight themselves. She towered over me. I stared up at her silhouette. The light shining through the window made her look even more like something out of a magazine. She was so fucking beautiful, and I was beyond turned on.

I could feel the heat from her inner thighs growing hotter and hotter, as she ground her body against mine. She started massaging my breasts until my nipples were as hard as hers. Then she proceeded to suck them with her soft, full lips; mixing a few bites in-between. She licked her fingers before using them to massage my lady button. I swear I felt like I was going to explode right there in the palm of her hand. I was dripping with lust. We started kissing fervently. Then, she spread my legs as wide as she could and began working her way up and down my body, placing sweet kisses all over me. Before I knew it, her face was buried. Tingling sensations rushed through my spine. She teased, and tugged, and licked until I swelled with unbridled passion. Then I couldn't take it anymore. I grabbed her hair and started force feeding her. She let me know she appreciated my aggression by plunging her tongue deep inside, as she continued to work her magic. Not long after that, the fireworks began; one explosion after another. It was amazing.

For months, Paige and I were all over each other. Every time we were in each other's presence, we were exchanging affection in some shape, form, or fashion. Yet, neither one of us was forcing anything to be. We both were just going with the flow. She was still my best friend, and I was hers. I knew Paige was still married and living with her husband-wife, but their marriage had been on the rocks for a long time.

Therefore, when Paige stopped voluntarily sharing details about her marital state, I stopped caring to know about it. I didn't feel the least bit guilty about our secret love affair. After all, Paige was in an "open" marriage.

Since Paige was always over at my place, I ended up giving her a key. It wasn't just because we were bedroom besties. However, it did make things more convenient. I loved coming home some nights to find Paige there waiting for me, with wine chilled and dinner going already. She totally spoiled me. That's why I feel terrible about how things ended between us.

When Paige was around, I didn't think about Greyson at all. She made me that happy. She was my friend, lover, and confidant; my friend more than anything though. I loved what we had. There was no need to put a label on it, and I most certainly wasn't trying to label myself. I knew that Paige classified herself as a lesbian. She had zero sexual interest in men. However, I felt like I was still a straight woman or maybe just an experimental bisexual. What I do know is that I loved Paige, because I loved Paige. I was attracted to her because of what she was to me and for me. It had nothing to do with her being a woman or the fact that she was super sexy. Well, maybe it did a little. Okay, fuck it. Maybe I am bisexual. But, I'm not a lesbian.

Although I hated most men at the time, I was still attracted to them; specifically, their cologne and their meaty man parts. Because of that, when Grey stopped by one evening, to bring me a check for the mortgage, I got one whiff of his Bleu Cologne by Chanel and instantly melted. I played it cool at first, but my insides were stirring up. Granted, Paige had been keeping me sexually satisfied. Still, there's nothing like the girth, the scent, and the feel of real veins, on the real shaft, of a real man; at least that's the case for me.

Before I knew it, Grey had me bent over the sofa. He was fucking the shit out of me; almost like he hadn't had any, in a while. Then, he picked me up and carried me to the bedroom. In there, he continued to pound me with relentless, yet welcomed, aggression. It hurt a little, but it felt so good at the same time. I was scratching his back, grabbing his head, and moaning like crazy. He was lost in the sauce, and so was I. Then, I looked over at the bedroom door, and Paige was standing there.

I haven't heard from Paige since she stormed out of my condominium that day. I was devastated that she walked in on Grey and me having sex, especially since I had just been rolling in the bed with her that morning. It's been months, and still, I can't get her to answer my calls or text me back. I pray that she's okay.

When I think about the happiness and rescue Paige and I found in each other, as we both dealt with broken hearts, caused by our broken marriages, it makes me miss her even more. I realize how much of a calm she brought to my stormy life. She made me happy. She made me smile. She kept me laughing, and she certainly kept me high and feeling worry-free. I don't know if I would have been able to deal with all the stress and shit that Grey put me through, had Paige not come along. Sometimes I feel like I would have ended up killing myself. That's a scary thought. I really think she saved me and I hate that I hurt her. It also makes me think about how many other women are out there, who might be going through the same thing and just need to be rescued.

Since I have nothing else better to do, I think I'll go back on Craig's List tonight, and put up another ad; just like the one I posted on the night I met Paige. Maybe she'll stumble upon it. Perhaps not. But if nothing else, maybe I'll find someone else like her.

Who am I kidding? You can't replace someone like Paige. She's rare. I guess I am too. Maybe I should just start a secret club for women like Paige and me instead; for women who get up and go to work every day and wear a smile, even though they're torn to pieces on the inside. I want to connect with those women, who on the surface, appear to be so poised and perfect. But, underneath it all, they're dealing with some real-life shit, day in and day out; like me.

My club will be a judgment-free, secret sanctuary for women. It'll be a place where we can come to lean on each other, vent, cry, and laugh. But, ultimately, a place where we can come to have a good time and release stress, or do whatever else it is that helps us cope with our life's lacks. I want us to feel free to just be. I want us to feel free to unleash our covert or taboo alter egos if we so choose. We can get drunk if we wish to. We can smoke weed if we want. We can even rent a man and go in the back and have a ménage a trois with him, if that's what we want to do. I don't care. I just want us to be happy, or at least feel happy, when we're together. We deserve that much. And it will always be understood, that what happens here, stays here.

Starting up this club may be the only way I'll survive this exceptionally shitty stage of my life. It may also be the only way that I'll come close to finding someone or something like what Paige and I had before. Because of that, I can't just let anyone in. There will be requirements. First, the club will only be open to women. Second, I prefer those who are professional business women, in some capacity. They can be teachers, doctors, secretaries, business owners, sales consultants or whatever. Their actual profession doesn't matter. I'm just looking for women who understand what it's like to get up and go to work every day, push through, and smile; even when secretly dying on the inside. Honestly, I kind of want the great pretenders; the ones who understand that everyone doesn't need to know everything about them. I can better identify with those types of women, and they with me. I'll even consider a desperate housewife or two. What's most important though, is that they each have something to lose and/or a reputation to protect. Ultimately, that's what's going to guard the secrecy and integrity of our club.

I'm sure the kind of women I'm looking for are out there; discreet, professional business women, dealing with broken hearts, and with life in general, just longing to be rescued. What I'm not so sure of, however, is how to reach them. I'm not too certain they're perusing the W4W section on websites like Craig's List. But hey, you never know. After all, it is how I met Paige.

I think I'll call the club *SCREETY*, which'll stand for *Secret Club Rescuing Every Emotionally Torn Yoni*. Members can be lesbian, bisexual, bi-curious or straight. It doesn't matter. They just have to be classy, discreet, open-minded, and fun to be around. No ghetto, ratchet-ness allowed. I'll be sure to emphasize that in my ad. In a week or two, I'll host a small meet-n-greet to get things going. Depending on the turnout, I'll do it again in a couple of weeks, and just take it from there. Either way, it should be fun.

Wow, I feel somewhat excited now. This will give me something to do to keep my mind off Grey and Paige. It'll be like I'm on a rescue mission, saving torn women; myself included.

10

Three weeks ago, I decided to just go for it. I decided to do something stark and unconventional. I decided to start a secret club for women. Not for all women though, but for a select group. The club would be for women like me; Screetys.

The response I got from my first ad was beyond anything I could have ever imagined. Who knew that there were so many torn, stressed-out, brokenhearted businesswomen in Atlanta with covert alter egos, who were just longing to be rescued. I certainly had no idea, but it was a refreshing discovery. It let me know that I wasn't alone.

Surprisingly, I received ninety-seven replies within twenty-four hours of posting my ad on Craig's List. That's not counting the annoyingly thirsty and perverted men who responded as well. Still, I could not have been more pleased. Although it was a bit overwhelming at first, messages continuously flooded my inbox, as I hastily tried to read them all, and decide on who'd get a response from me first. As tedious as it was, I must admit that it was also very empowering and satisfying as well. The level of keen interest I received had me feeling like a boss.

As planned, I posted my first recruitment ad under the women for women section, on Craig's List. In addition to making SCREETY the acronymic name of my club, I also decided to turn it into a word that generally described the type of women I was looking for. My ad read:

Are you a Screety?

If you're a professional businesswoman (or housewife) with a covert or taboo alter ego, and you use it to help you quietly deal with whatever bullshit life throws your way, AND you know how to have fun, **"discreetly,"** *the answer is YES!*

I'm a teacher, a closet bisexual (as of recently), and I have been separated from my husband for about two years now. He lied. He cheated. And did some of everything else in-between. It's been a lot to carry. That's why I'm here. I want to start a secret club for other women, like me, to help us better deal with the headaches and heartbreaks we quietly cope with every day. Let's have cocktails, relax, and just help each other enjoy life a little bit more. No, you don't have to be separated or divorced. It's perfectly okay if you're married or in a relationship. No, you don't have to be bisexual. It's perfectly okay if you're lesbian, bi-curious, or straight. However, there are seven things you **MUST** be if you'd like to be a member:

1. a **WOMAN (no exceptions)**
2. **Discreet (what happens here, stays here)**
3. **Open-minded (not judgmental)**
4. **420-friendly (even if you don't indulge)**
5. **Classy, but fun to be around (let your hair down)**
6. **A business professional or business owner (housewives will be considered)**
7. **NOT loud, ghetto-acting or "ratchet" (self-explanatory)**

*I will be hosting a private meet-n-greet soon, with lots of food & adult beverages. If you are interested in attending, and you meet ALL the above requirements, **please reply with a pic** and tell me a little bit about yourself. Also, you will be required to* *voice-verify over the phone, before receiving an invitation to the "Screety" party. I look forward to hearing from you all. Smooches;)*

That was my ad. Nothing too over-the-top, but fancy enough I guess. I wasn't sure if it was going to work, but it did. Forty-two ladies RSVP'd, and thirty-eight of them actually attended SCREETY's first meet-n-greet. There could have been more, but I had to be conscientious of the catering-n-cocktail budget since I was paying for everything. Therefore, everyone who expressed interest didn't necessarily get an invite; at least not this time around.

The night went off without a hitch. We laughed, ate, drank, played fun icebreakers, and really got to know each other. I think we all made several new friends that evening. For me, each lady was a gem. Two, however, were especially dazzling. One's name was Logan, and the other, Symone. Ironically, both reminded me of Paige, in their own unique way.

Logan's personality was so like Paige's that is was eerie. She was smart, flirty, and amusingly sarcastic. She was also very attractive. Her eyes were a beautiful amber. They totally complimented her orange-red hair, which she wore in a cute, layered, asymmetrical bob. And, just like Paige, she smoked weed; every day.

Learning that Logan enjoyed indulging in the "good stuff" was refreshing; especially since it was my new thing too. Before Paige stormed out of my life, she kept a big zip-lock bag, full of weed, in my freezer. She never came back for it. At first, I didn't want to touch it. Her big bag of weed, hidden inside an old Starbucks Pumpkin Spice coffee pouch, had sentimental value. It probably also remained untouched, because I didn't know how to roll a blunt or a joint. But, after a while, I said "fuck it," and learned how.

It didn't take long for me to figure out how to roll a decent joint. After that, I pulled a fat nugget or two from Paige's stash every day. Smoking weed had proven to be a major de-stressor for me, so I wasn't trying to stop. It became a part of my night-time regime. After I'd finish grading papers, and doing whatever else I needed to do to prepare for work the next day, I'd shower, pour a cocktail, and smoke a joint. I called it my puff-puff-and-pass-out regime.

Yes, Paige and Logan were so much alike; from the way they rolled a blunt, even down to the way they laughed. I couldn't believe it. However, there was one big difference about them; Logan was white.

I actually met Logan a couple of weeks before my party. She and I ended up meeting at a trendy bar for happy hour, about a day or two after replying to my Screety ad. She even helped me plan our first Screety gathering. I loved her vibe from our very first phone conversation. Maybe the fact that she also worked with children had a little something to do with that. It was that night, at the bar, when I learned that Logan was the owner/director of a very prominent child care facility in Atlanta, Georgia. However, that was only the beginning. I soon learned much more.

Logan had a fun, organic spirit about herself. She spoke with great articulation and sophistication, but playfully used slang words without hesitation. It didn't seem forced though, or like she was trying to impress me. In fact, her apparent mix of racial influence came across quite naturally and inoffensively. It all made sense when she told me she was married to a black man. They had two children together. I think Logan expected me to have funky feelings towards her interracial marriage. I'm sure she's had more than her share of eye-rolls from black women. But, it wasn't a big deal to me. Love who loves you, as far as I'm concerned. Shit, I had my own marriage and relationship problems to worry about.

I could hear a sigh of relief escape from Logan's breath when I smiled, after she showed me a few pictures of her husband and kids on her phone. Her family was beautiful, and I told her so. I also told her that they looked so happy and perfect. She smiled back, but quickly responded with, "Well, looks can be deceiving." I understood exactly what she meant. With that, we lifted our glasses and toasted to meeting each other, and to our finding someone who simply "understood."

After two Long Islands and one shot of tequila, I learned a lot more about Logan, and she about me. First, I learned that her husband was a former NFL player. He played for the Atlanta Falcons. Since I'm not a huge football fan, I didn't recognize him, nor his name. Tragically, his football career ended a few years ago, when he suffered a major, irreparable injury. Luckily for him and Logan, they'd made some wise investments beforehand, Logan's childcare facility being one of them, so they were still financially stable. Logan told me that she and her husband first met while attending college in Alabama. They had been married for twelve years. In fact, he surprised her with an elaborate trip to Vegas about a month ago, to celebrate their wedding anniversary.

She talked a little bit about her kids and shared their ages. She told me they were ten, seven, and two. I didn't recall seeing any pictures of the third, and youngest child. So, of course, I inquired.

Logan had been babysitting her Long Island for the past hour. It was now completely watered down. But, before answering my question, she slurped it all the way down through her straw; leaving only a few melted ice cubes at the bottom of her glass. After shaking her glass a few times, to make sure there was nothing left to sip, she told me the youngest child wasn't hers. He was her husband's.

I just stared at her. I couldn't find the words to respond. It immediately triggered a sadness within me; that's exactly what I was trying to avoid. I told Logan she didn't have to say anymore. Then I ordered us another round. Thankfully, the bar had a nice DJ in the mix. He kept the party going. The music was certainly a welcomed distraction. To lighten the mood, Logan and I just started dancing and playfully twerking in our high-top chairs. We got back to talking and laughing; about other, less heavy, stuff. Although I stopped Logan from expounding on her husband's crushing indiscretion, I knew that she was aware that I completely understood her pain. And I think that was enough for both of us.

11

Have you ever seen or met someone for the first time, and instantly assumed they'd be one way, personality wise or whatever, and they turned out to be the complete opposite? I've certainly been guilty of it, more than a time or two. It's always invigorating though, to be pleasantly surprised when they don't live up to your subpar expectations. Instead, they exceed them, leaving you in awe; completely blindsided. That's pretty much how it all played out when I first met Symone.

With all the responses I received from my initial Screety post, it quickly became time-consuming to read all the emails, reply, exchange pics, and voice-verify the many ladies who had expressed interest. While it was fun, it was certainly cumbersome. Additionally, since I knew I could not invite everyone to my first event, I found myself inviting the more attractive women and skipping over the not-so-pretty ones. Then, I came across Symone's email.

At first glance, Symone's email was a complete turn-off. It was five paragraphs long! I was already tired and was only looking for the ladies to tell me a little bit about themselves, and attach a pic; not detail their life story. I was tempted to delete it, without even reading it. It just seemed like way too much was going on with it, right off the bat. I mean five paragraphs, really? For me, it felt like the lady behind the email was a little too desperate, and a little too broken, because she had a little too much to say.

Before deciding on whether to trash the email or to just come back to it later, I noticed that Symone had at least followed instructions, by attaching a picture of herself. Not everyone had. They made it easy for me to skip over them. So, if nothing else, I figured I'd at least take a quick glimpse at her pic. That's when I saw that she had attached multiple pictures, so I just clicked on the first one. That was enough, because what I saw floored me.

Symone was a big girl! Although, there's nothing wrong with being a big, full-figured girl. In fact, the extra pounds can be quite womanly and sexy, if carried well. However, Symone was super plus-sized, and kind of sloppy-looking too. She didn't carry her weight well at all. It was mostly in her stomach; like a big sack of potatoes stuffed inside a kangaroo's pouch. How dreadful is that for a woman? If I had to guess, I'd say she was over three hundred pounds, and she couldn't have been much taller than me.

It wasn't that I was judging Symone because of her weight. Well, maybe I was, subconsciously. Either way, I didn't feel like she would be a good fit for the club. Based on her appearance alone, I assumed that she couldn't possibly have any real business credentials or any alluring sophistication about herself, and certainly no husband. I assumed that she was lazy. Therefore, not particularly the type of woman I wanted to be associated with. Part of me even felt like she should expect to have her heart broken, repeatedly, in her quest to be loved by a man or a woman. Not because she deserved it any more than I did, but because the world is a pot of shit. If you're fat and/or unattractive, life is going to be a little harder for you. People aren't going to be as quick to like you or love you, but they'll always be quick to judge you. That's just the way it is.

I could only shake my head as I stared at Symone's picture. There she was, stuffed into a red, ill-fitting skirt suit, standing in front of what appeared to be a library, ankles swollen, hair braided in two thick plats, looking like an old lady. But even with all that going on, her round face and features made it evident that she wasn't an old lady. She was clearly in her late twenties or early thirties. Still, I could only cringe as I envisioned her showing up to the Screety party....

She'd look a mess, like she didn't belong. For the most part, she'd be quiet and reserved. She'd probably be too torn, depressed, and/or sexually deprived to relate to the other girls' conversations or to be of much fun. Her excess girth would likely cause her to have an unsettling body odor; one that she's had for a long time, but doesn't notice anymore. Ultimately, it would cause the other ladies to feel uncomfortable. So, they'd slyly distance themselves from her. Mostly, Symone would spend the evening sitting in an isolated corner of the room, just quietly observing. By the end of the night, her greatest sense of fulfillment would come from indulging in half a glass of wine and hitting the Mexican spread, laid out in the kitchen, at least three times. That's how I envisioned it.

Now, I have done some things in life that I'm not particularly proud of, and having those immediate, judgmental thoughts about Symone is one of them. Having said that, just as I was about to close out her email, still without reading it, I remembered why I was hosting a meet-n-greet in the first place. It was to rescue other emotionally torn women because I was torn. I understood what it felt like. So, how could I not even consider trying to rescue Symone? That went against my whole mission. Because of that, I read her email; all five paragraphs. When I was done, there was one thing I knew for sure; I had to meet her.

When it came down to it, I repulsively prejudged Symone. Shamefully, I couldn't have been more wrong:

Hello,

My name is Symone. I came across your ad on Craig's List, and I think what you're trying to do is great. To answer your question: Yes, I am a Screety. Funny, I didn't know that I was one, before today- lol. I think this name you've come up with, to describe ladies like us, is really cute. It's quite fitting too. Oh, I also saw that you have seven requirements, to become a member. Well, I'm happy to say, I meet ALL of them! Yaaaaay! I would love to join your club. Will there be a fee required to join? If so, I'm happy to pay it. But first, let me tell you a little bit about myself: I'm 32 years old, with no children. Not yet, but hopefully one day. I currently live in Decatur, Georgia with my husband of four years and I'm a ten-year librarian. I know, not the most exciting career-lol. But, I love what I do and I also love to read, so it fits me. I'm a bookworm, unquestionably.

In my free time, I like to, you guessed it, read books - lol! I don't get out the house very much, except for attending my book club meetings and going to church. My life is BORING! Please save meeeeeee!

Now, let's talk about my alter ego; though it's not very exciting either- lol. First, I love to drink wine. I know you're probably thinking, "Okay, so what?" But, most who know me, don't know that about me. My family and friends have pegged me as the "good girl," all my life, so I just play into. More so for them, than for me. Plus, my husband doesn't allow me to drink outside of the house anyway, even when I'm out with him (which is rare these days). He says it's un-lady-like. Therefore, I drink wine at home, A LOT; and alone. I'm almost always drinking alone because my husband is hardly ever here. He works in sales, so he travels a lot. That's part of the reason I drink so much these days. I'm depressed and lonely.

Two years ago, I was diagnosed with Cushing's Syndrome. It was said to have been caused by a tumor. The tumor has since been surgically removed. Still, the condition persists ☹. There's actually more to it than that, but I'll spare you the details. Ultimately, as a result, I've gained over 100lbs. The pain and weakness I often experience in my legs forces me to walk with a cane most days. Hence, why I'm in the house so much. I've tried some of everything to lose the weight, but haven't been very successful. However, because of my weight gain, it's obvious that my husband isn't attracted to me anymore. I'm sure he's found someone else, and I think he's just buying time or maybe he just doesn't want to give up the beautiful home we recently purchased. I don't blame him. I know I don't look the way I did when we got married, just four short years ago, so I understand. Still, it hurts.

The second thing I do covertly, that absolutely NO ONE knows about, except for my husband (and now you), is smoke weed. That's because it's my husband's weed that I smoke. He always has plenty in the house. He'll usually roll me up a few blunts and leave them in a zip-lock bag, before disappearing on one of his many two-day excursions, disguised as business trips. I'm certain he's with some raggedy skank each time! But, what can I do? I just feel helpless and hopeless. Getting high at least helps me sleep through the night, most of the time.

How's that for a librarian... and her alter ego? lol

Anyhow, I don't want to go on and go. I know this message has been long enough. But I hope to hear back from you. Until then, take care. Oh, and I attached pics too.

Regards,

Symone

Before replying, I had to sit for a few minutes and take in all that Symone had shared. I felt so bad for her. I felt even worse after clicking on the other pictures she'd attached. In them, she looked nothing like the girl I saw in the first picture. She was gorgeous. Her figure was amazing, curvy, and voluptuous. And as aforementioned, she was about a hundred pounds lighter. She looked happy and healthy, unlike in the first. Those subsequent pictures were clearly of who she used to be. My heart couldn't help but hurt for Symone. The only thing I could think to do was try to be her friend, by helping her find a few drops of sunshine again. But mostly, I couldn't wait to get high with her.

12

It's been four months since my first Screety party. I've hosted like eight more since then. Honestly, it feels like a second job now, but in a good way. I'm a teacher by day and a club president by night. Yes, SCREETY is now officially a real-deal club; with designated officers, paying members, and everything. I'm having the time of my life! So much so, that I've almost forgotten about Paige. Okay, let me stop lying. I haven't. I can't. In fact, with all the fun I've been having, it makes me wish Paige was here even more. She would be the life of the party.

Last night, Logan and Symone came over to finalize the details for our next event. After much deliberation, we decided we're going to have a stripper-themed party! All the attending members took a vote, at our last get-together, and the stripper theme won by a landslide. I thought that was hilarious. But hey, my girls know what they want, so we're going to give it to them! With my dream team and me, aka Logan and Symone, in charge of planning, it's guaranteed to be a shit load of fun.

All the Screety parties, before this upcoming one, have been exhilarating and fun. Still, we felt it was time to turn things up a notch. Usually, I have my condominium set-up as a relaxing oasis for the ladies. Scented candles are burning everywhere. A nice playlist is going in the background. Food, wine, and alcohol are plentiful. I even have a designated, well-ventilated smoking room; equipped with multiple air-purifying, smoke-filtering machines and plenty bottles of D.A.T. Spray. The ladies love popping in there to take a few tokes, without having to worry about the smell of weed or smoke lingering in their hair or on their clothes.

Typically, we spend the evening playing drinking games, doing karaoke, and having some major heart-to-heart venting sessions. The more we drink, the deeper they get. We've all shared some painful secrets about our individual lives. I love the fact that we seem so comfortable exposing our private pains and struggles with each other, without fear of being judged. I've heard some things from these girls that have made me cry, that have made all of us cry. But, believe it or not, the crying helps; so does the alcohol, and definitely the weed.

So far, we've hosted all the Screety parties at my place. It only makes sense to keep that trend going, especially since most of the other ladies don't have the space in their home or they don't live alone.

Hosting at some rented public venue is also out of the question, especially one that would require additional money. We want to make our club's current funds stretch as far as they can. Two, being in a public space would take away from the obscurity of the club. The ladies wouldn't feel free, to just be.

Still, my three-bedroom condo is starting to reach its capacity for hosting our events. Now that we have over seventy members, it's becoming more challenging to squeeze everyone in; comfortably. Luckily though, everyone can't make it to every party that we host, so that helps. According to Symone, who serves as the club's Secretary, we now have seventy-two members. Even better, Logan, our Treasurer, shared that all members have paid their $50-a-month club membership dues, in full, to date.

We've been using the money to cover the cost of food, drinks, alcohol, marijuana, hookahs, decorations, and entertainment for our parties. As part of the SCREETY membership agreement, we've promised to host at least two private, members-only parties, every month. All members are welcomed to attend and indulge in all offerings, at no additional charge, if their membership dues have been paid. So far, it appears that all the ladies feel as though they're getting their monies' worth. I'm glad about that.

I chose Logan to act as the club's Treasurer because she was so willing to contribute her own time and money from the very beginning. Although I fully funded the first party, Logan certainly helped me coordinate things. Then, for the second party, she contributed half of the money to cover the costs, and wouldn't take no for an answer. After that, we took

Symone's advice and incorporated a monthly membership fee.

For this next event, we'll really be tapping into our budget. But, since we have close to $3600, just from this month's dues alone, I think we have more than enough to cover the cost of having a really good time. For starters, we're going to bring in a few pole dancing instructors. They'll teach us how to dance like the sexy strippers that our current and past lovers love so much; like the exotic dancers some of us openly and secretly love too. We'll have the instructors spread out and set-up in different rooms, to ensure everyone gets a chance to learn a trick or two. Then, for the second half of the party, we're going to bring in real-life strippers; male and female. They'll serve as our entertainment! One of the male dancers that Logan recommended, allegedly has a

12.5-inch penis. I can't recall how she knows about him or the dimensions of his sausage, but I'll have to see it to believe it; up close and personal, with my own set of eyes. Because of that, Logan got no objection from Symone or me, regarding Mr. Hung Kung. We're looking forward to the showcase.

When Logan left, Symone stayed. She said she needed to talk to me. I could tell something had been on her mind most of the evening, though she tried her best to hide it. Before she got into what was on her mind, she asked if I could refill her glass of wine. The three of us had just about killed the box of Riesling I'd cracked open earlier in the evening.

When I returned with Symone's glass, I noticed she was trembling. It made me nervous. I asked her what was wrong and she told me it was her husband, Brandon. He had texted her out of the blue, about an hour earlier. His message read, "I'm going to fuck you up when you get home." It scared Symone, so she immediately excused herself from the dining room table, where she, I, and Logan had been sitting, and stepped outside to call her husband. She called him five times, back to back, but he never picked up. Then she texted him, but he didn't reply. That's when she knew she was in trouble.

I knew that Symone's husband had been both verbally and physically abusive towards her in the past. That was something she'd shared with me, in confidence, when we first met. She told me that no one else knew about it, not even her family. Since it was something that didn't happen very often, by her definition, she didn't feel it was too big of a deal. According to Symone, a few scuffles with her husband wasn't worth having folks all up in her business. Foolish or not, she didn't want her marriage to end behind it.

By Symone's recollection this evening, Brandon hadn't violently put his hands on her, in more than a year. However, she accredited that to him being so wrapped up with his alleged side-chick. In Symone's mind, he was so into his greasy side-piece these days that he didn't even care to cuss her out anymore. Before, he'd badger her daily, about being too fat. And occasionally, he'd beat her up, for forgetting to take the trash out. Now, he rarely did either. Sadly, to Symone, that's what confirmed that he didn't care about her anymore. I swear, the more she talked, the more I hated the son-of-a-bitch she'd married. Still, more than anything, I was scared for her.

Symone had told Brandon that she would be at a book club meeting tonight. That's what she had been telling him, each time she came over for a Screety party or one of our meetings; even though she hadn't been to an actual book club meeting in months. Yet and still, it wasn't an issue. Brandon never questioned her about her whereabouts. Her social life had consisted of the same old boring things for years; book club, church, and an occasional Sunday dinner with her family. Because of that, Brandon had no obvious reason to worry. Plus, he was never at home to verify anything, anyway. It wasn't like he was ever there waiting on her, just to discover that she was already drunk or high when she arrived. Brandon rarely even called Symone. When it came down to it, he didn't give a fuck about her; not anymore. Honestly, I doubt he ever did.

From what Symone could gather, she hadn't given her husband any reason to suspect that she had been lying about or hiding anything. So then, why was he so upset and threatening her tonight? We both sat there trying to think of what it could be. I even grudgingly asked if she had remembered to put the trash out on curb this morning. Then, when she stood up to adjust her pants, it came to me.

When Symone and I first met, four months ago, she was really depressed. To me, her weight was the biggest reason, for more reasons than one. Combined with her illness and her husband's decreasing desire for her, Symone had pretty much let herself go. She had stopped caring about how she looked. Then, not long after we met, she started to care again.

She asked if I could help her shed a few pounds by being her personal coach/accountability partner. I happily agreed. After that, I gave her an old Fitbit of mine and encouraged her to get in 10,000 steps a day, on the days that she could. I also pushed her to cut most of the sugar from her diet and to drink more water. It worked. In this short amount of time, she's lost close to fifty pounds. Additionally, I convinced Symone to spice up her hair a bit too. Since she's into more natural styles, the other day, she got her hair braided in long Senegalese-twists. They're gorgeous. With the weight loss and the new "do," Symone has been looking more and more amazing each day; like she's found happiness again. Unfortunately, I think her husband may have noticed it too.

13

It was parent-teacher conference night at school today. So, without any additions, my day was already going to be long. What made it feel even longer though, was that I could not stop thinking about Symone. I was worried about her. I hadn't heard from her in two days. Considering the hostile text message, she'd received from her husband the other night, while at my place, I feared that she wasn't okay.

While meeting with my students' parents, I kept my phone close by. Since it was on silent mode, I was glancing over at it, every few minutes, to see if a call or text had come through from Symone. By six o'clock, I figured I wouldn't be hearing from her today. I was too afraid to call or text her again, thinking her husband could have possibly had her phone. The last thing I wanted to do was make things worse for my friend.

After wrapping things up at school, I made my way to my car, and prepared to head home. Before I could pull off, my phone rang. It was Symone. She didn't have much to say. She only asked if I had made it home yet. I told her, "No." But I added that I would be there in about thirty minutes. Her only response was, "I'll meet you there." Then she hung up.

Two minutes after I walked in the door, my doorbell rang. I couldn't get to it fast enough. I just wanted to lay my eyes on Symone and actually "see" that she was okay. However, when I opened the door, I immediately realized that she wasn't.

Symone's hair was different. It stood in disarray all over her head, like she hadn't bothered to comb it today. Also, she clearly had a busted lip. It looked like she'd tried to cover it up with deep burgundy lipstick. That didn't work though. Her battered lip was quite obvious. I hugged her, then quickly yanked her inside the door. I must have asked if she was okay, like twenty times, before she made her way to the sofa to have a seat. Then, I asked if I could get her something to drink.

"He said I left an ink pen in his pockets when I washed his clothes the other night. Apparently, I ruined his favorite pair of jeans, along with a few shirts. Blue ink got all over them," Symone began. I sat across from her in silent disbelief because I knew where the story was going. "He beat the shit out of me!" She continued. "Then, he demanded that I immediately take the ugly ass braids out of my hair because I hadn't gotten his permission to get them done, in the first place. But, before I could, he just started snatching braids straight from my head, by their roots. It hurt so bad!" She softly cried as she patted her freed hair. "After that, he made me sit there and finish taking all the braids out of my hair, one by one, until I was done. It took six hours! Blood was all over me," she finished.

I didn't know what to say to Symone, other than, "Let's go kill this motherfucker right now!" But I knew that wasn't an option, so I didn't say that. Instead, I asked, "Where does your husband think you are right now?" She told me he had flown out to Las Vegas for a sales convention, and wouldn't be back for a few days. He had called her from his hotel room, shortly after checking in. Apparently, he wanted to make sure she was doing okay. He also wanted to apologize, again, for losing his head a few nights ago. From what Symone expressed, her husband hadn't inquired about her whereabouts; not today, not tonight, or any of the nights before. But, since it was Wednesday, she supposed, that he assumed, that she was just at church; for bible study.

Since Symone's visit was somewhat impromptu, I didn't have a chance to grab anything for dinner. Luckily though, I found some salmon filets in the freezer, so I was able to hook up some nice Cesar salads for us. Subconsciously, I was still trying to keep Symone on track with her low-carb diet. So, instead of wine, I made us vodka spritzers with a splash of fresh lime juice and club soda, to keep the car-count low. They were nice and strong. Just what we needed.

After dinner, Symone pulled a nice, fat blunt out of her purse. I could only shake my head as I smiled and gazed at its size. Without a doubt,

Brandon was riddled with guilt when he rolled that blunt for Symone. In fact, he rolled four others just like it. She couldn't resist showing me the stash bag that he had left for her. Clearly, Brandon wanted Symone to get higher than the cost of living, and just forget about everything that had happened.

Symone and I unquestionably took a trip to the moon; and back. We had our cocktails. We played some music. We got high as shit. But no way could we forget about what had happened. Although, Symone wanted to just forget about it, but I couldn't. And I couldn't let her. While I was still struggling to find all the right words to say, no part of me could take the domestic abuse, which had been inflicted upon her, lightly.

Symone pointed out that she couldn't even comb her hair, because her scalp was still sore and covered in scabs from where her husband had ripped the braids out of her head. The visual that played in my mind was horrid. I had to excuse myself a few times, just so I could go to the bathroom and cry.

When the weed and alcohol settled in, completely removing my filter, I couldn't keep from asking Symone the question I had wanted to ask her for the longest. "Why the fuck are you still with this negro?" I blurted before I knew it. Since she was just as buzzed as I was, Symone only answered my question, with a question. "Why are you still married to your husband on paper, even though he's been gone and living with another woman, for over two years now?" she countered. My first thought was, *You bitch.*

I laughed off Symone's question because I certainly didn't want to talk about Grey's ass.

However, I did acknowledge that she had made a good point. While I have my reasons for not having finalized my divorce yet, honestly, the reasons aren't good enough. And I know that. I need to get it done. Still, I want Symone to understand the seriousness of her situation. It isn't just about a cheating husband, in her case, it's much bigger than that.

Symone's staying with her husband jeopardizes her safety and well-being. I don't think she gets that. When it comes down to it, her fear or tolerance could cost her everything. She needs to leave him; plain and simple. This isn't just about love or lust. I believe, for Symone, it's inevitably, about life or death.

I know Symone doesn't want her family and friends to know her dark secrets. She wants everyone to think her life is pure and perfect, outside of her illness, of course. But, part of the problem is, her husband knows that too. Brandon's confident that Symone would never say anything to anyone; not about what's really going on in their marriage. In his mind, Symone would never leave him nor betray him. She'd never do to him, what he's done to her.

Like an opportunist, preying on someone's insecurities, Brandon is taking advantage of Symone because she's weak. Correction, in the past she's been weak; physically, mentally, and emotionally. Her husband knows it, and I know it too. However, I've been trying to help Symone gain her strength back, and just feel better about herself again. Unfortunately, her husband doesn't want that for her.

Being the savage beast that he is, Brandon will continue to verbally and physically abuse Symone, until he is forced to stop. He knows Symone tolerates his abuse and neglect because she doesn't think she deserves any better. And if she does think she deserves better, she probably doesn't think she could ever really have it.

At the end of the day, Symone will just keep pretending like everything's okay, even though it isn't. She'll never voluntarily expose the truth to her family, friends, or co-workers. In her mind, it simply isn't their business. When it comes down to it, she's a discreet and private woman. She's a Screety. We aren't quick to share or expose our personal business. We always pretend like everything is "a-okay," at all costs. Yep, that's what we do; we pretend. I just pray that pretending doesn't cost Symone her life.

14

We should have just gone with a Vegas theme for our party, opposed to the stripper theme. Not that the stripper theme didn't fit, because it did. My goodness, gracious, it really did! But, with all that happened at our Screety party over the weekend, you would have thought we're amongst the bright lights and anything-goes kind of nights in Las Vegas, Nevada. I don't know if I'll even be able to look some of these girls in the eye again. I'm kidding. Still, all that happened here definitely must stay here!

The best part of the night, without a doubt, was Mr. Hung Kung. He was definitely in the building; all 12.5 inches of him! Logan had been most accurate in her description of him. He was tall, dark, and bearded; with the most beautiful set of white teeth that I have ever seen. His body was chiseled to perfection. He smelled like chocolate and amber. And his rich baritone voice, alone, could make you melt into a puddle. But, back to his penis, that thang was HUGE!

Strong, healthy veins lined every inch of Mr. Kung's man tool. It was impossible to resist touching it. That's why we didn't resist. About fifty ladies attended the party. I think we all got a dance from him. He was incredible, and I'm sure, quite tired, by the time he left us.

We ended up bringing in a total of four strippers; two men and two women. First, there was Alexis. She was a cutie pie. She had short, platinum blond hair, and piercings all over. Her nose was pierced, as well as her tongue. She had enormous breasts. They were only complimented by the two erotic piercings through her nipples.   But, Alexis didn't stop there. To top it off, her clitoris was pierced too, with a shiny silver hoop. Most of the girls hadn't seen anything like it before, not in person. They were quite fascinated and impressed.

Next, there was Harmony. She was tall and had the most flawless pair of legs. They stretched for days. Her ass was amazing too. I later learned that she loved to sing. Hence, her stage name. She graced us with a few melodies over the course of the evening. I made it a point to let her know that I was a part-time songwriter. I even asked if she would consider recording one of the songs I'd written. She was on board without any hesitation. Still, to make things more appealing, I also shared that my husband was a big music producer in Atlanta. I never gave her Grey's name though, and didn't feel the need to point out that he was my "estranged" husband either.

Carlito was our other male stripper. He was sexy as shit. His shoulders were nice and broad. His skin was smooth and nicely tanned, like a buttery almond spread. He also had a great smile. I couldn't get enough of it. But, best of all, Carlito was packing! Although his man muscle wasn't as big as Hung Kung's, it was still a nice, long piece of machinery. I couldn't wait to get my hands on it.

By the time our entertainment arrived, the Screety ladies and I were already quite "lit," as the kids say. We were dressed in scanty clothes, lingerie, and high heels. Everyone played along with the theme. Our exotic dance instructors had given us a real work out earlier that evening. Still, we were fired up. In between taking turns grinding and twirling on the poles, we all had been sipping, and most of us had been smoking too.

Sexiness and sensuality floated throughout my condo. Something about that night really brought out the ladies alter-egos. I was just happy to see the girls letting their hair down like they never had before. After all, the Screety Club was where they could come to do whatever they wanted, however they wanted, and with whomever they wanted. And man, oh man, did they!

It all started when Heather, one of the attorneys in our group, decided she wanted to put on a show for the ladies. She borrowed one of the instructor's poles and set it up in the center of the living room. After that, she selected her song. It was an oldie, but goodie, by Nas. It featured Ginuwine. The name of the song was, "You Owe Me." As soon as the beat dropped, we all just starting hollering like school girls. The familiar melody immediately took each of us back to a particular moment in our life. A time when we were younger, and perhaps felt freer and happier.

Heather's figure is no joke. She's a well-known gym junkie and her tight physique reflects it. When she began her dance routine, sporting red stilettos and a tiny black negligée, I had no idea what was about to go down. But, she quickly showed us; everything.

For the first forty-five seconds of the song, Heather popped, dropped, and worked the hell out of that pole. It was as though she had done it many times before. She impressed the ladies so much that some started throwing dollar bills at her. Most of us had cash tucked in our bras for the strippers who would be arriving later. Then, after Kanil, who was seated in the love chair, threw a hundred one-dollar bills at Heather, the turn-up got very real.

Heather made her way over to Kanil and stared down at her seductively. Kanil's big brown eyes gazed back. Then, just like that, Heather disrobed; in front of all of us. For a few seconds, she just stood there naked, as the playlist continued to go in the background. I couldn't believe my eyes. I don't think any of us could. However, one thing we all agreed on, Heather's body was even more astounding in the nude. And her tits? Yes, they were perfect too.

Kanil is a doctor. She completed her residency program not too long ago. She's always been one of our more quiet and conservative members, but still fun to be around. In fact, she recently graced us with THE best weed any of us has ever had. She'd gotten it from a marijuana dispensary in Colorado. Being a doctor and all, she has access to buy weed, legally.

I didn't know what to think, as Heather stood before Kanil, with her pom-pom in her face. I was hoping Heather hadn't gone too far, making Kanil feel uncomfortable. But, before I could say anything, Kanil grabbed Heather by both ass cheeks and pulled her down into her lap. After that, the two spent the next thirty minutes or so, groping and kissing all over each other. Now, I think they're quietly dating.

With the lights low, candles glowing, and music playing, Kanil and Heather set off a domino effect in the room. A lot of the ladies started dancing all over each other. Some were even kissing. A few had decided to take off their bras as well. Even those not into the girl-on-girl action were having fun. So was I. I was even turned on a bit. Nonetheless, as much as I tried not to think about Paige, I couldn't help but think about her. It was impossible not to, especially after watching Kanil and Heather practically drown each other in saliva, then duck off into the guest bathroom. I can only imagine what all went down in there. Because of that, I couldn't stop thinking about Paige. I missed her and nobody there could replace her. That kind of killed the arousal thing for me.

The strippers arrived around ten o'clock. We were beyond ready for them, especially Logan. She was drunk. There's no other way to put it. I know for sure that she'd had at least six shots of tequila, plus a glass of wine. Logan, without a doubt, was white-girl wasted. Thankfully though, she had already planned to spend the night.

As the exotic dancers performed for us, we fondled them and cheered them on like a bunch of guys at a frat party. I noticed though that Logan was being extra attentive to Mr. Hung Kung. I even overheard her ask if he remembered her. I don't think he did. But I'm certain, following Saturday night, he'd never forget her ass.

When it was time for Mr. Hung to take center stage, Logan personally cleared the way and escorted him to the middle of the living room floor. He came dressed in black leather pants, a white, button-down shirt, and a matching leather vest. His biceps were exploding. The first thing he asked, was for volunteers to help him get undressed. All the ladies were willing, but he could only choose four. Lisa, a marketing director, helped him get out of his vest. Amber, a hair salon owner, unbuttoned his shirt.

Joleen, a dentist, removed his belt with her teeth. And last, but not least, Logan, our treasurer, helped him get out of his pants.

It was like we had discovered a pot of gold, and it laid there in his crotch. His thong underwear was a shimmering gold, in fact, and it just barely covered up his over-sized penis. As Hung Kung made his way around the room, thrusting, gyrating, and collecting lots of cash, we all pleaded for him to let us see it in the flesh. Not long after, he honored our request.

Returning to the center of the room, Mr. Hung asked Logan to come up. Then he told her to get on her knees. When she did, he pulled out his dick. It looked like one of those big, black dildos you see in an adult toy store. It didn't seem real. We all sat there in dripping-awe as he slowly began to stroke it. He teased us with every inch. We watched, without blinking, as it grew bigger and harder.

The show went to another level when Logan reached up and started helping Mr. Hung masturbate. For a moment, we all envied her. Then, without warning, Logan started sucking his dick. It was a pretty amazing thing to see. She was quite skillful. I don't know how in the hell she managed to do it, but somehow, Logan fit his entire 12.5-inch dick into her mouth! At first, I thought I was just seeing things. Because, I too, was very much under the influence. She was gagging a lot to get it down, which is understandable. But, we cheered her on, and somehow, she did it. Not only did Logan fit the entire massive piece of meat into her mouth, but she sucked on it, until he came; right in her mouth. I was slightly appalled at first. But, based on Logan's reaction, it was exactly what she wanted. So, if she was happy, I was happy. No judgment here.

Overall, it was a great night. Although, Logan did spend the rest of the night throwing up, before passing out on the sofa. A few other girls slept over too. For those who had to get home, but were a little too tipsy to drive, I had them leave their cars, and just got Ubers for them. We always made sure our girls were good.

If nothing else, all the ladies had fun and were highly entertained that night. I love it. I've managed to create this stress-free oasis, where women can escape and feel free. That makes me happy. Ultimately, I want to rescue every woman who needs it. Speaking of which, Symone couldn't make it to the party. She had to cancel at the last minute. Apparently, her husband came back in town early.

15

I'm holding off planning any Screety parties this month. There's just too much going on. I don't think having a party or a club meeting is the remedy; not this time.

When Symone couldn't make it to our last event, it didn't sit right with me. She had put so much time and effort into helping us plan it. Then, when she told me her husband had come back in town early, I felt like there was more to the story than that. Soon, I learned there was.

Symone pulled another disappearing act. After a week went by, and I still hadn't heard from her, I made my way to the library where she worked. I left work early that day, just to check on her. When I got there, I didn't see her right away. It made me nervous.

Then, just as I was about to leave, I spotted her putting books away in a back aisle.

She was noticeably smaller and her hair seemed thinner. I didn't rush towards her. Instead, I waited for her to look up and see me. When she saw me, her eyes lit up with a sense of relief. She discreetly beckoned for me to come over to where she was standing. We gave each other a quick squeeze. I immediately noticed that Symone seemed pained when I touched her back as I hugged her. I asked her about it, but she just brushed it off.

Since we were in the middle of a library, we couldn't converse very much. Symone told me to go to the front desk and request a key for one of the empty conference rooms. She said she would meet me there in ten minutes. I got the key, and I waited. My heart was pounding a thousand beats per minute.

After about twenty minutes, Symone tip-toed into conference the room. She sat down very gently. Again, like she was in pain. "Are you sure you're okay?" I asked. "About as okay as I'm going be," she replied. "It's just the Cushing's Syndrome. Sometimes it causes me a little discomfort, but it's not a big deal," she added. I didn't believe Symone. I felt like she was hiding something. While I had read up on some of the signs and symptoms of Symone's disorder, I didn't know all there was to know about the condition or disease. Still, I believed her husband had more to do with her pain than anything.

"Why haven't I heard from you Symone? You had to know I was worried about you." I pressed. She couldn't even look up at me, to answer. Then her hand started trembling. I placed mine over hers. She looked me in the eye, and the tears just rolled.

"He took my phone," she whispered. "He took the keys to my car, and he has been whooping my ass, with a belt, every single day, for the past two weeks." Symone detailed. "I think he wants to kill me," she said.

"One day, when Brandon was at the grocery store, he ran into one of the girls from my book club. Without thinking, she told him to tell me that my presence was missed at the book club meetings. Adding, that they hadn't seen me in months," Symone continued. "Now, Brandon thinks I've been sneaking around with some other man," she closed.

So, the maggoty son-of-a-bitch was beating her ass and holding her hostage because of his own torrid insecurities. He had already stripped her everything. She had nothing left. Symone was living in fear. I wanted so badly for her to call the cops or at least tell a family member what was going on. But, I couldn't force her to do it. I also didn't want to overstep my boundaries. Symone had to first want to remove herself from the deadly situation. Until then, I couldn't do anything.

By the time our brief chat ended, all I could see was red. My mind had switched to gangster-mode, though I'm the furthest thing from it. I felt like Cleo in "Set It Off," minus the cornrows. "Fuck this shit! You know what you gotta' do. You have to swiss-cheese this motherfucker, and I'm going to help you do it. If we don't kill him, he's going to kill you. There's no doubt in my mind." Then, I walked out. Those were my last words to Symone, last Tuesday.

16

Just when you think you're over someone or a situation, life has a fucked-up way of reigniting it, all over again. I accidentally discovered something today, and I swear I wasn't looking for it. Well, at least I didn't start out looking for it. Either way, I found it. Now I'm right back at square one; hurt, disgusted, and confused. I can't believe this happening. I can't believe I'm here; again.

There's a reason I stay off social media sites. They make me sick. All the fakery, all the people pretending that their life is so much better than it is, gets on my nerves. Plus, I can't take folks, I barely even know, being all up in my business. However, today, I decided to reactivate my Instagram account temporarily. I was only compelled to do so because I was caught up in a moment of boredom, and I hadn't heard from Grey in a while. I wanted to see what he was up to.

The last time I saw my husband, or even spoke to him, was about six months ago. He was coming over to drop off some money for the mortgage. When he arrived, he was surprised to discover that his key no longer worked. I had changed the locks. It pissed him off. He felt that since he was still paying the mortgage, he should have access to the condominium, whenever he felt like it. I disagreed. After all, it was his fault that we were in the situation that we were in.

Long story short, he never gave me the money that day. He told me that if I needed to change the locks, I needed to figure out how to pay the mortgage on my own. For three months, I did just that, thanks to money I had in my savings account. I never bothered to call him or text him. Nor did he ever try to reach me. Then, around the fourth month, I received a check in the mail from Grey. It was equivalent to six payments. Attached, was a sticky note that simply read: "*For mortgage.*"

When I first went to his page, I immediately realized that I had been blocked. That let me know he had something to hide. My heart raced as I quickly created a new, fake Instagram page. I had to know what he was hiding. I was hoping his page was still public, so I wouldn't have to send a follow request. Luckily, it was.

The first thing I noticed when I went to his page were countless pictures of his daughter. She's gotten big. Then I noticed in many of his recent pictures, he was pictured with the same woman. Her face looked familiar, but I couldn't recall how I knew her or even if I knew her. I just knew it wasn't Tiffany's bitch-ass. I began clicking on the pictures one by one. They confirmed that the chick pictured with Grey was someone he was now dating. She was very attractive, so I couldn't but feel some kind of way.

The more I clicked on pics, the more disgusted I became. Then I noticed he had tagged his lady friend in one of the pictures. So, I clicked on the tag, and it took me right to her page. What I saw, killed me all over again.

She and Grey had just welcomed their new baby boy into the world! He was born on Grey's birthday and weighed 8lbs, 7oz. If that rusty dagger didn't cut me deep enough, the fact that she referred to Grey as her fiancé, was wearing an enormous engagement ring, had tagged Grey in the pic, and his commenting back with the kissy-face emoji did.

I felt my soul leave my body. I had to take a moment to process everything. My first thought was to send @littybae1027 a direct message, and ask her when exactly had she become engaged to MY husband. However, I decided to wait on that. I needed to have a conversation with Grey first, tonight.

I tried calling Grey several times. As expected, he didn't answer. I left him a voicemail, and followed-up with a few less-than-pleasant texts. He didn't respond to those either. That only infuriated me even more. After revisiting his Instagram page, I learned that he planned on being at Magic City tonight, so I planned on being there too.

I knew I had to be incognito. I had to be discreet. I didn't want Grey to spot me before I spotted him. He'd go out of his way to dodge me for sure. I couldn't let him see me coming. I couldn't let him know I was there, not until I was ready to confront him.

In preparation for the evening's events, I took to my closet to find something to wear. I knew my outfit had to be unassuming. I needed to wear something that would allow me to blend into a strip club environment quietly. At first, I couldn't think of anything. Then, I remembered these costume accessories that Logan, Symone, and I had purchased, for a future Pimps-n-Hoes themed Screety party.

It took a while, but I finally put together the perfect undercover ensemble. I was going to be a dirty-south stud, with a minor feminine twist. I slicked my hair back into a bun. Then I put on a black pair of jeans with a black hoodie. To keep from looking like I was coming in there to rob somebody, I topped my outfit off with hot-pink, high-top sneakers. The best touch of all though, was the faux set of full-grill, gold teeth that I'd found in our Screety-party stash bag. They were the perfect touch. I slid them over my teeth, brushed on some hot-pink lip gloss, and put on a pair of jet-black Oakley shades that once belonged to Grey. I was all set and ready to go. Nobody was going to recognize me. Then, my doorbell rang.

17

It was like she had just seen a ghost. Her pupils were dilated. Her eyes were swollen, possibly from crying or from fighting. She was very much out of breath and struggling to breathe. Perspiration had gathered on the tip of her nose and raced down the sides of her face. She smelled like the outdoors; as if she had run all the way here. I didn't know what to think. I just knew Symone looked like a monster.

I got her some water before I said or asked her anything. She was just as perplexed by my appearance, as I was by hers. "Did I catch you at a bad time?" she asked. "No, not all," I replied as I handed her a glass of water. "Ummm, are those gold teeth in your mouth?" Symone persisted. I knew I was going to have to explain to her why I was dressed, the way I was dressed, but I needed to find out what was going on with her first.

Symone told me that Brandon had been dropping her off at work, and picking her up, ever since he had taken her car keys some weeks ago. However, he didn't show up today. Symone assumed that he had forgotten that the library would be closing early today since it was Friday. After calling him several times, to no avail, she decided to just take an Uber home.

When she got home, she saw that both cars were in the driveway. That alone, wasn't a big deal. She figured Brandon had taken a nap, and just overslept. However, when she walked through the front door, she immediately heard that he was wide awake.

Symone made her way upstairs, careful to tread lightly. Then, she stood just outside her bedroom door and watched as her husband made love to another woman. She said she didn't make a sound. She couldn't. After a minute or two, she'd seen more than she could stomach. So, she quietly crept back downstairs, got her car keys off the counter, left the house, and drove here.

That explained why she looked the way she did. Her heart had just been ripped from her chest. She had undoubtedly cried the entire way here. I quickly replaced her glass of water with a glass of wine. After that, we sat and continued talking about the day's events; including my own.

Symone decided that she wanted to roll with me to Magic City, to confront Grey. She'd never been to a strip club before, but was curious to see what it was like. Like me, she needed to be in disguise. Luckily, Fridays are casual-day at the library, so Symone already had on a pair of jeans and sneakers. That made it easy. I just grabbed one of Grey's old sweatshirts for Symone. Then, I hooked her up with shades and gold teeth, just like me. She even put on some hot-pink lip gloss. As we stared at ourselves in the bathroom mirror, we couldn't help but laugh.

I was nervous as shit about confronting Grey. So, when Symone and I pulled into the club's parking lot, we decided to park and fire up a blunt before heading inside. I had to shake the jitters. Since we were trying to be undercover as we stalked Grey, we had to make sure we didn't attract any unnecessary attention. We knew the smell and sight of weed smoke could easily do that. To avoid it, we didn't crack the windows. We just hot-boxed my truck and used D.A.T. Spray to kill the smell. Symone and I were ridiculously high by the time we headed inside.

With our gold teeth and shades on, I'd almost forgotten that Symone and I looked like a pair of tom-boys. The strippers flocked to us, as soon as we walked through the door. I'm not sure if it made Symone uncomfortable at first. But, if she was, she didn't show it. She was in character. Therefore, I put my game-face on and joined her. I figured we'd just make the most of the night and have fun, despite our detriments.

I ordered us drinks. I got us table dances. We even enjoyed some spicy hot wings and fries. Given the circumstances, it was a fun night. We laughed and lived it up. However, after being there for a couple of hours, there still was no sign of Grey. It's expensive to keep a table, at a strip club, on a Friday night. I'd already spent over four hundred dollars on parking, admission, dances, drinks, and food. It was almost time for us to call it a night. Before we left though, I thought to check Grey's Instagram page for any useful updates. When I did, I learned that he would not be coming; not there, not tonight.

Symone and I made our way back to the car. We couldn't wait to snatch the gold teeth out of our mouths. She couldn't stop talking about how much fun she'd had. I was happy for her. I was elated that I could show her a good time; she needed it. However, as we drove back to my place, her whole demeanor changed. I assumed it was because we were back to reality.

I told Symone she didn't have to go home. I insisted that she spend the night. I was fearful of what might happen to her if she returned home, especially so late.

Her husband had proven to be a deranged lunatic. Still, Symone insisted that she had to go, even though I begged her not to.

I practically came to blows with Symone, to keep her from leaving my house tonight. Before she left, I screamed, "What the fuck is wrong with you? Do you want to die?" Her response was devastatingly chilling. She chuckled, then shook her head and said, "I'm already dead, and so is he. I killed him."

18

I'm not sure when she came by, but when I awoke this morning, there was a hand-written letter from Symone inside my door. After the bombshell she dropped on me, just before leaving my house two nights ago, I was almost afraid to read it. But, I had to. I'd been seeing her face all morning. She was headlining news. Symone had been charged, in the murder of her husband and his mistress. She turned herself in. I'm still frozen. None of this seems real to me. Please wake me now, if it isn't.

Dear Noel,

How shitty is life? Well, you already know my answer. One thing I want you to know though, is that I am so grateful I met you. You, and the Screety Club, have given me sunshine where there was once nothing but darkness.

I know I kept some things from you and I'm sorry, cause you were the only one in the world that I could talk to. My family and friends distanced themselves from me a long time ago, because I chose my husband over them. They saw who he was from the start. I just chose to ignore it.

The other thing I've been reluctant to share, is that I have cancer, and it's terminal. That's the real reason I've been losing so much weight. No one else knows this but you. According to the docs, I have about two months to live, which is perfect. That means I won't have to sit in jail very long. Hopefully, it'll also give me just enough time to get my life back right with God, so I can go to heaven.

One last item, I have a $200,000 life insurance policy and I've added you as the sole beneficiary. I knew I'd be leaving soon. The last thing I wanted was for that *dirty dog, and his side bitch, to be living la vida loca, off my money. Well, clearly that's not an issue anymore. Plus, I'd rather you have it. Go throw the biggest Screety party you can think up! Stay on your rescue mission. I love you Noel. Thanks for the good times and thanks for rescuing me. Now, go roll up!*

Symone

I felt like I had been hit by a freight train. I tried to think of anything I could have done differently, to save her. My heart felt so empty and defeated. I just needed to lay down and cry.

As I was making my way to my bedroom, the doorbell rang. It startled me. I wasn't expecting any visitors. For a second, I feared it was the police. When I peered through the peep-hole, I still couldn't decipher who it was. They didn't look threatening, so I opened the door.

In a million years, I wouldn't have guessed that my day would have started and ended the way it did. I probably hadn't been sadder, since the day my mom died and I hadn't been happier, since the day I married Grey; before it all went bad. When I opened the door and saw her face, I couldn't believe my eyes. It was Paige. All I could do was stand there, stare, and cry.

The End

Noel's Song Diary

(to be recorded & released by various artists at a later date)

Number One

Number one implies that there's somebody else
But I'd rather be the one than by myself
And I know that all my friends may not agree
But, right now I gotta do what's best for me
Cause they just don't understand
All the long nights I spend, and I can't sleep
Tryna get over you
After all we've been through, I can't leave

I love you too much
Time invested in us
Yes sometimes it gets rough
That's ok baby
I don't care what they say
They don't know how I've prayed
And I won't walk away

As long as I'm number one babe
You can go and have your fun baby
I won't question you about what you do
As long as I'm number one babe
You can go and have your fun baby
Just show you're in love with me
I'm content with being number one

When I think of all the things we made it through
I'm convinced that you're for me and I'm for you
Even though we've had our share of real bad days
I wouldn't trade it at all

No, not for anything

I love you too much
Time invested in us
Yeah sometimes it gets rough
That's ok baby
I don't care what they say
They don't know how I've prayed
And I won't walk away

As long as I'm number one babe
You can go and have your fun baby
I won't question you about what you do
As long as I'm number one babe
You can go and have your fun baby
Just show you're in love with me
I'm content with being number one

The time it takes to cuss and argue
Is time wasted cause I still love you
I've been worried bout the wrong thing
So let'em say what they want
It don't matter
Turn off your phone
I won't sweat it
At the end of the day
I don't care what they say
Cause I know this one thang
You coming home to me
You coming home to me
Oh yes, you coming home to me

As long as I'm number one babe
You can go and have your fun baby
I won't question you about what you do
As long as I'm number one babe
You can go and have your fun baby
Just show you're in love with me
I'm content with being number one
Number one
Number one...

Life Goes On

I fell in love with you
On the very first day we met
And I was so confused
And things I can't forget
Why did you have to do
All the things you did to me
Cause you made it hard to see
That I ever would be free

But I let you go
Even though I knew
It would tear my heart away
Felt so by myself
Seemed like nothing helped
Thought I'd throw this life away
Oooooh, yes

But just when you think it's over
Really it isn't over
Life goes on, (hey)
And you can get pass the bad days
Troubles may come but won't stay
Life goes on

So I just keep telling myself
Whatever happens
Whatever happens
I, can't let it get the best
Won't let it get the best of me

Whatever happens

So I let you go
Even though I knew
It would tear my heart away
Felt so by myself
Seemed like nothing helped
Thought I'd throw this life away
Oooooh, yea

Cause just when you think it's over
Really it isn't over
Life goes on,
And you can get pass the bad days
Troubles may come but won't stay
Life goes on

Sometimes the hurt and pain
Builds up inside
And you can't do a thang
But sit and cry
But I want you to know
You gotta let it go
Use it to make you strong
And move on
Move on

Cause just when you think it's over
Really it isn't over
Life goes on
And you can get pass the bad days

Troubles may come but won't stay
Life goes on
(It ain't over, hey... It aint over, hey)
Life goes on
(It ain't over... It ain't over)
Life goes on...

Clean

Somebody say a prayer for me
Cause I'm drowning now
I'm blind and I can't see
How I'll make it out
But then an angel said to me

He still loves you
And he will come and make you clean, yea
Your past don't matter
Cause in His blood he'll make you clean
And it don't matter what has happened in between
Cause I know I've done things I wish she didn't see

Yea I know what I did
And I know I messed up
Yea I fell on the ground
But I'm trying to get up
May have slept with one or too many men
Really needed the money so I did it again

And now, the walls are closing in
Don't know which way to go
It seems like I've been right here in this place ten
times before
I swear my heart beat pounds so fast and sometimes
it's slow

So, somebody say a prayer for me
Cause I'm drowning now

I'm blind and I can't see
How I'll make it out
But then an angel said to me

He still loves you
And he will come and make you clean, yea
Your past don't matter
Cause in His blood he'll make you clean
And you might end up places you just can't believe
But you will make it through if only you believe

Cause it's never too late
And you're never too gone
Yea I know it looks bad
But you gotta hold on
Say it to yourself over and over again
No matter how it looks you gotta know you can win

And no,
Doesn't matter what you did
Doesn't matter how you live
Doesn't matter what it is
He'll make you clean, he'll make you clean

God help me,
Cause I'm drowning now
I'm blind and I can't see
How I'll make it out
But then an angel said to me

He still loves you

And he will come and make you clean, yea
Your past don't matter
Cause in His blood he'll make you clean…

At the Drop of a Dime

Tell me your every wish

Tell me your commands

I'm doing everything I can

To make you see

I need you here with me

But it's so obvious

That you still wanna leave

Baby, tell me what it is I gotta do

I've worked

I've cried

I've prayed

And stayed for you

In between everything

That's what true love means

It means too much

For you to up

And walk away

At the drop of a dime

You just wanna pack your bags and leave

But I won't let you go so easily

At the drop of dime

At the drop of dime

At the drop of a dime

You wanna walk away, way, way

Please stay, stay, stay with me

Cause I won't let you go

Not that easily

At the drop of a dime

At the drop of a dime

At the drop of a dime

You wanna walk away...

You're still in love with me

Tell me it ain't true

That's why I'm down to fight for you

But first you need to see

You belong here with me

Yet it's so obvious

That you still wanna leave

Baby, tell me what it is I gotta do

I've worked

I've cried

I've prayed

And stayed for you

In between everything

That's what true love means

It means too much

For you to up

And walk away

At the drop of a dime

You just wanna pack your bags and leave

But I won't let you go so easily

At the drop of dime

At the drop of dime

At the drop of a dime

You wanna walk away, way, way

Please stay, stay, stay with me

Cause I won't let you go

Not that easily

At the drop of a dime

At the drop of a dime

At the drop of a dime

You wanna walk away...

Decision

We started talking

And at first it didn't seem like

You really had too much to say

Look I don't really want it

Cause I don't really need it

But it's hard for me to walk away

Never felt so bold

But now I'm feelin' bout it

You can keep on playing games

And soon you'll be without it

Look at what you did to me

Yes it's still hard to believe

But oh,

Somebody's gonna break your heart

Somebody's gonna do what you did to me

So obviously I,

Just gotta find a way to tell you goodbye

And Oh,

Somebody's gonna break your heart

Somebody's gonna do what you did to me

And when the reaper comes

Look, we gotta make a decision

But hurry up before it's too late

Too late, too late, too late

Ooops, it's not an illusion

Cause now I think you waited too late

Too late, too late, too late

But fuck it, here the reaper comes…

I.D.G.A.F. Anymore

I'm so sick of trying to be the one
I will let you just go and have your fun
Imma let'em all think what they want

I'm not gone worry if you don't call
Cause I know I have been through it all
I'm sick and tired of being strong
I'm sick and tired of holding on

Now, I don't give a fuck anymore
Oh I don't give a fuck anymore
No, I don't give a fuck anymore
Cause I'm tired of trying to be
Some things aren't meant to be

So, I don't give a fuck anymore
No, I don't give a fuck anymore
Oh I don't give a fuck anymore
Cause I'm tired of trying to be
Some things aren't meant to be
So I'm done.

Tried my best to forget and forgive
But loving you makes it hard to live
It's crazy, but I won't let it kill -me

I'm not gone worry if you don't call
Cause I know I have been through it all
I'm sick and tired of standing tall

So now I'll just let it fall.

Cause, I don't give a fuck anymore
No, I don't give a fuck anymore
Oh I don't give a fuck anymore
Cause I'm tired of trying to be
Some things aren't meant to be

Now, I don't give a fuck anymore
No, I don't give a fuck anymore
Oh I don't give a fuck anymore
Cause I'm tired of trying to be
Some things aren't meant to be
So I'm gone...

Basically I...

The good times have been good

But they'll never outweigh the bad

And though you may never see it

I think I'm kinda glad

Cause soon I'll have the peace

I've been without so long

Ain't no need to tell your story

Cause baby I'm already gone

And basically I

Don't think you were meant for me

And I'm not meant for you

And basically I

Can do bad by myself

Don't need no help from you

And basically I

I'll be ok

I'll make it anyway

Basically I

Am moving on

I gotta away

I'm moving on

I gotta go away

You don't love me like you should

Constantly make me sad

After all I've done for you

You could at least feel bad

But soon I'll have the peace

I've been without so long

Ain't no need to tell your story

Cause baby I'm already gone

And basically I

Don't think you were meant for me

And I'm not meant for you

And basically I

Can do bad by myself

Don't need no help from you

And basically I

I'll be ok

I'll make it anyway

Basically I

Am moving on

I gotta away

I'm moving on

I gotta go away...

Stuck on the Bad Side

I know, I know, I know

You don't have to tell me

Cause I've been here before

I've been locked up and locked out

Broken and abused

No matter what, I was always seem to lose

And every time I tell myself

This time I'm through, it never happens

It never happens

And no matter what I do

No matter how I change

Bad luck seems to follow me

It always seems to rain

And I think I just might lose it all

Probably go insane

Kinda kooky-crazy

And really hard to explain

Cause I'm,

Stuck here on the bad side

Send and SOS for me

I'm, stuck here on the bad side

And it won't let me leave

I'm, stuck here on the bad side

Send an SOS for me

I'm, stuck here on the bad side

It's got a hold on me

I've been drugged up and drug out

I've been so confused

He broke my heart so much, now it's split in two

And every time I told myself

This time I'm through

It never happened

It never happened

And no matter what I do

No matter how I change

Bad luck seems to follow me

It always seems to rain

And I think I just might lose it all

Probably go insane

Kinda kooky-crazy

And really hard to explain

Cause I'm,

Stuck here on the bad side

Send and SOS for me

I'm, stuck here on the bad side

And it won't let me leave

I'm, stuck here on the bad side

Send an SOS for me

I'm, stuck here on the bad side

No it won't let me leave...

What the Heart Wants

The minutes feel like hours

And the hours feel like days

And even though you're probably over me now

I cannot say the same

I tell myself, why bother

You're not in love with me

But it's a matter of the heart

That my mind just fails to see

Cause the heart wants

What the heart wants

And the mind can't tell it no different

No, no, no, no, no, no

Cause the heart wants

What the heart wants

And the mind can't tell it no different

I'm longing every hour

Wishing to be with you

But I know that you've moved on now

Still my heart longs for you

I tell myself, why bother

You're not in love with me

But it's a matter of the heart

That my mind just fails to see

Cause the heart wants

What the heart wants

And my mind can't tell it no different

No, no, no, no, no, no

Cause the heart wants

What the heart wants

And my mind can't tell it no different...

The Grey Area

Somewhere in the grey

Somewhere in the grey

Maybe if I count back from ten I will feel better all over again

Sometimes I tell you to go

Then I fear that it's the end

I can't really see where we fit

But it's really hard to just quit

I gotta find a way to let go

And wet my feet up

You say you had enough

And I'm just fed up

But all I do is cry when you go away

I just really wanna know where we stand

Cause I really can't be your girl, you can't be my man

And there's really no way that we can just be friends

Still it's really hard to tell where it is we both belong

It's been going on

I guess we're just lost in the grey,

In the grey, in the grey area

In the grey, in the grey, in the grey area

We're just lost in the grey, in the grey area

Maybe we'll never ever find our place

Colors change and fade

Guess it's where we'll stay

In the grey area, in the grey area, in the grey area

Really looks like we're lost here in the grey

So in the mist of this my life goes on

Got other issues I'm dealing with so I must be strong

The rain pours, the wind blows, can't catch a break

At any given moment it may take my breath away

Some seem so highly favored

But I can't seem to win

Wish I could start all over

And try my life again

Cause I can't stand the pressure

Don't know which side to choose

You call it, heads or tails

Either way, I'll probably lose

I'm lost, I'm lost

And I'm really searching for direction

The cost, of bad decisions lasts forever

Or at least that how it seems

So many things have happened,

Not sure what they mean

Cause we're lost in the grey,

In the grey, in the grey area

In the grey, in the grey, in the grey area

We're just lost in the grey, in the grey area

Maybe we'll never ever find our place

Colors change and fade

Guess it's where we'll stay

In the grey area, in the grey area, in the grey area

Really looks like we're lost here in the grey

I know that things will get better

I know we'll figure it out

Cause I done made through so many storms now

I ain't gotta reason to doubt

Hope the sun comes out and shines its rays

And with new light we will find our way

But if time goes on and things don't change

Don't worry bout it, at worst,

You'll just be stuck with me

Lost in the grey,

In the grey, in the grey area

In the grey, in the grey, in the grey area

We're just lost in the grey, in the grey area

Maybe we'll never ever find our place

Colors change and fade

Guess it's where we'll stay

In the grey area, in the grey area, in the grey area

Really looks like we're lost here in the grey

Grey grey, grey grey

It's grey, it's grey, it's grey

Grey grey, grey grey

It's grey, it's grey, it's grey

But it gets better

Yes, it gets better,

Yea, it gets better

Yea it gets better

Lost here in the grey...

Want to actually hear these

songs written by Dakota Jack?

Follow Dakota on Instagram & Snapchat!

@dscreety

www.dakotajack.com